A charming man with ravishing looks and a sharp eye for beauty in its myriad forms, Nicholas was born and raised in the Middle East, and is widely travelled, affording him a greater perspective on other cultures and the manner in which they differ from his own. Some of his stories draw inspiration from his voyages of discovery, and he continues to develop his creative mindset – a melting pot of different philosophies and perspectives – in order to best represent his characters.

Having studied ancient books of Arabic wisdom, and relating the stories therein to daily life, Nicholas has been able to gain a profound understanding of the human brain, and deeper insight into people's concerns, desires, passions, and their other innermost thoughts. He seeks to find undeniable truths in his accounts of human interactions, infusing them with authenticity and validity, while taking his readers on exciting journeys that explore the impulses, motivations and other emotions that make us who we are.

This book is for anyone out there who may relate to the feelings presented in this book but for one reason or another cannot admit this openly and be their true self.

Nicholas Pearson

FEELINGS OF THE MOMENT

Flames of Hidden Passion

AUSTIN MACAULEY PUBLISHERS™
LONDON • CAMBRIDGE • NEW YORK • SHARJAH

Copyright © Nicholas Pearson 2023

The right of Nicholas Pearson to be identified as author of this work has been asserted by the author in accordance with sections 77 and 78 of the Copyright, Designs and Patents Act 1988.

All rights reserved. No part of this publication may be reproduced, stored in a retrieval system, or transmitted in any form or by any means, electronic, mechanical, photocopying, recording, or otherwise, without the prior permission of the publishers.

Any person who commits any unauthorised act in relation to this publication may be liable to criminal prosecution and civil claims for damages.

This is a work of fiction. Names, characters, businesses, places, events, locales, and incidents are either the products of the author's imagination or used in a fictitious manner. Any resemblance to actual persons, living or dead, or actual events is purely coincidental.

A CIP catalogue record for this title is available from the British Library.

ISBN 9781398483408 (Paperback)
ISBN 9781398483415 (Hardback)
ISBN 9781398483439 (ePub e-book)
ISBN 9781398483422 (Audiobook)

www.austinmacauley.com

First Published 2023
Austin Macauley Publishers Ltd®
1 Canada Square
Canary Wharf
London
E14 5AA

Introduction

It is an oft-repeated phrase that 'the eyes have it'. So much is conveyed in a glance, however fleeting. Whether you are passing someone on the street or find yourself in a transitory meeting of eyes above a well-thumbed novel on the Tube; the complexity of a character and perhaps, even, a glimpse of a life lived to the full can be communicated with more eloquence than a thousand words. But the eyes are never more expressive than when conveying the emotion of desire.

What is so often unspoken and left simmering beneath the surface can find its outlet in a longing, lingering glance, for the body has its own language; one that can sometimes be at discord with the words that come from our mouths or the beliefs we have inherited from those around us; and which, with time and repetition, take hold in our minds.

This is a book that explores the conflict between the body, with all of its lustful, cursory passions, its mercurial and ever-changing longings, and the mind, which holds the animal desires imprisoned within the barriers of social expectation and inherited societal mores.

Society dictates that unfaithfulness to our partners is wrong. That if we look at, or even desire another person, we are morally abject, and failing as human beings. But these beliefs do not allow for those feelings that arise in a moment, when two bodies are drawn together by an inexplicable and, sometimes, inescapable lust. Are people simply following the impulses of their desire meant to be judged? Are they to be thought of as 'wrong'?

Where do our beliefs about what is 'right' and 'wrong' even come from, anyway? And why must we swallow these beliefs unquestionably, applying them to our lives without thought? These are the questions that have plagued me over a lifetime. Through my own life experiences over the years, I have come to believe that what I have been taught about 'right' and 'wrong' has failed to ring true for me in practice. The simplistic divider of people into Camp Right versus Camp Wrong does not allow for those in-between states – those which we are reared to regard as strange, but which I believe to be the most natural, primal states of being – when we are fully led by and invested in our feelings and feeding the needs of our bodies as they arise. When we are hungry, we eat. When we are thirsty, we drink. When we are tired, we rest. And when we are on fire with desire for someone, we should allow our bodies to merge with wild abandon, revelling in, and satiating, our sexual proclivities.

But we do not. Not always, and not whenever we want to. And why? Because we have been taught that to do so is wrong. To have sex with anyone we want is wrong. Especially if we are in a committed relationship – then it is incredibly wrong, sinful, and even unforgivable. It is a commandment given by God, after all: Thou Shalt Not Commit Adultery.

People find themselves in relationships for a variety of reasons. Sometimes, the relationship offers everything they think they want – companionship, friendship, security, a family, the sense of a milestone being reached. But perhaps there is a part of them, barely acknowledged, that it fails to fulfil. Occasionally seemingly 'good' relationships lack that fiery, primal element; that spark between two people that can roar into unbridled, dripping passion ... and a life without this element is, I believe, a life only half-lived. Yes, it is a safer life, a gentler life, without it. But that does nothing to assuage the open space its absence leaves in someone's life; a gaping emptiness that, whether acknowledged consciously or not, aches to be appeased. Nature abhors a vacuum, and in no other area does this vacuum long more urgently to be filled than in the area of unsatiated carnal desire.

If such a need continues to go unmet for an extended period of time, it can lead to frustration. Such feelings can rise to the surface in a variety of ways. Perhaps the husband is distracted by work or lacks confidence in the bedroom. Whatever the reason, there is a disconnect between husband and wife, leaving a problem that needs to be resolved. And then, when this problem remains unsolved, the powerful emotion of desire persists, pulsing beneath everything in the wife's daily life. And where do all of these unfulfilled desires go?

In my experience, there are certainly situations in which cheating – which is so often vilified, point blank, in our society – can not only be a positive thing, but a saving grace for people stuck in relationships that fail to give them full bodily pleasure. From when I was young, I found myself drawn into situations as the third party, or 'other man'; but, far from causing chaos and heartbreak, I found my involvement with other people's women to be hugely beneficial, not only to the sex-starved women themselves, but also to their men, who, once their women had their desires fulfilled elsewhere, were able to soften towards their partners; to be kinder to them, more understanding of their situations, and more accepting of their character, and whatever work and life stresses they were under. As a result, they tended to be more satisfied with their lives overall.

Each real-life story laid out in these pages in explicit detail elaborates on my own personal philosophy. I believe that acting upon the desires that arise in those fleeting moments, when two charged glances connect, can often be the best thing for everyone involved, whether either person is married or not. Sometimes these situations arose because the woman was sexually unfulfilled by her partner, and sometimes not. In each case, the common thread was the electrifying moment when our eyes met, that split second in which the wave of lust reared up above us both and came crashing down, and the inevitable hunt for desire that connection sent me on, resulting in the gradual erosion of my conquest's every bastion of morality against their desire for me.

Do I see myself as a saviour or helper of unfulfilled women? Perhaps. I do believe in discretion and see it as unnecessary for someone to 'come clean' to their partner out of guilt. Such revelations would only cause unnecessary pain, when, if they are kept secret, can benefit both people, by giving each of them what they need, but cannot give one another. The missing piece that a person cannot find in their otherwise adequate relationship is found, allowing the other aspects of the relationship which do work, which are successful, and which are compatible, to flourish.

The following stories are based on my own experiences, teaching me all about the power of desire, and how a mind ensnared by lust cannot help but yield to its need, regardless of the situation. The feelings that arose between me and another man's wife were momentary, in many ways volatile, and ultimately transitory, but the impact upon us both was lasting.

This book centres on two topics. Firstly, the feelings that, as quick as the flick of a switch, disregard all other emotions in favour of unrestrained passion, compelling a woman to act against all principles, and societal restraints inherited from all religions, mothers, aunts and sisters. Secondly, how that passion is extracted once identified, overlaying and maybe even replacing the small-minded, limiting mindsets that prohibit sexual freedom of expression.

I now invite you to make up your own mind, as I present a collection of stories that demonstrate how impulsivity can cast aside long-held tradition in favour of passion.

Chapter 1 – Debbie

Back in the '60s and '70s, life in the Arabian Gulf was not easy. Poverty was rife, and there was little knowledge about the outside world. Manners and traditions controlled everything, and any foreigner would be called English, no matter where they came from. Very few families were able to travel and, if they could, Egypt or Lebanon was their most likely destination, while most did not own a car – and if they did, it was restricted to one vehicle.

The country was just starting to develop, and most engineers were foreigners. For that reason, most parents wanted their children to study abroad, to become engineers capable of building the nation.

Sexuality was simply a sin, and a woman was like hidden treasure. Their bodies were totally covered, and the only glimpse a man could get of them was via a small strip of bare skin around the eyes, which they obscured with a veil as they passed through a market. Even the magazines imported from abroad would have female bodies blacked out with markers, leaving only a pale, rectangular square around the eyes.

If a man saw a girl's face, he would fall in love with her immediately, and body shape didn't play a role in those times whatsoever. There was a real struggle for those spontaneous lovers as there were no telephones back then so you wouldn't know what to do and how to reach your flame. Phones only started becoming widely available in the late '70s, easing the lives of many.

As teenagers, when we gathered at night, we mostly talked about sex. Of course, a lot of what we spoke about was lies, but we liked it. When somebody saw a girl, he told us stories about him kissing and touching her, and sometimes even making love to her. Our brains pulsed with activity whenever we heard these lies, and we also talked about studying in the USA, and how women there loved black-haired men with brown skin, and that this alone would compel them to have sex with us.

TV was very strict, and no woman's body would be shown on it. There were two channels – English and Arabic – and sometimes you saw a woman in tight jeans or a short dress, and that image would linger in a teenage brain for weeks, acting as fantasy fuel and all but obliging him to touch himself.

Maybe that is why Arabs became very good at reading eyes and interpreting what could be in someone's mind, just by looking into their eyes. For sure, I was good at that, and soon became renowned for it. In my small little town, I was almost the Prince of Teens back then.

When I graduated from high school, I had good grades, which meant I was entitled to a scholarship from the government. It had long been decided that I would go to the United States. My parents were so happy, but I could tell it was not easy for them to let go of me; though they could foresee a future in which I took care of them in their dotage. They gave me their blessing, which made me very happy, and

I started to prepare for my overseas adventure, with two things in mind: learning English and having sex.

After collecting a great deal of information about the state in which I would be staying, and my accommodation options, I had to decide whether to stay in a student dorm, rent my own apartment, or stay with a family. I knew that staying with a family would improve my English and help me learn faster.

On the plane there, thousands of thoughts darted around my head, conjuring images alluding to my destination and, of course, the women there. A good 80% of my ruminations revolved around women, as I had been told that America was a free country, with easy-going girls. I knew, and had every confidence in, my talent, and was fully equipped with my wisdom, coupled with my ability to read people's eyes from one look.

It was late August when I reached Colorado, and I stayed in a small hotel, ready to start my new life. I reminded myself how assured I was of myself and my capabilities, and was ready to dominate anybody's mind and exert my influence over them; to control them but in a good, loving way. I loved adding positive value to people's lives and making a difference, and I was raring to go.

After checking into a hotel, I took a taxi to the English learning centre I was to attend. I knew it was close but wanted to know the location and see what it looked like. The vast distances between anywhere of interest persuaded me to stay in my room until the next day, before going to school. It was about nine hours' time difference between Colorado and my country, so sleeping was not easy and I started playing with the TV. I found that I could buy and watch porn movies – many of them. At the beginning, I was a little hesitant to do so, because the hotel management would be able to see what I had been up to when looking at my bill ... but, still, I could not help it. I was so desperate to watch porn for the first time, and that night I came four or five times before going to sleep.

The school term was to start in a week's time, and I was to take a test the next day to determine the level I would be studying at. The same day, I was taken to meet the family I would be staying with, to see if they would accept me and whether I would like them.

It was a small household, comprising a mother, a father and their daughter, who was away, studying in New York. The husband was a man in his fifties, called John. His wife was named Debbie, who was around 40 years old. Debbie was a housewife and was at home all day, keeping the house in shape, and preparing the meals. John worked at a Kmart in sales. Each day, he left to go to work at about seven in the morning, and every evening he liked to sit in the living room, complaining about his boss, while downing beer after beer in front of the television. John loved to drink. He was not an alcoholic, but he drank an awful lot.

This seemed to irritate Debbie, who often made snide comments about his habits, or rolled her eyes whenever he opened another bottle. By comparison, Debbie, who was younger, seemed to look after herself well. She had a beautiful body, and was slim, with large breasts that she enjoyed accentuating with tight blouses and dresses. John and Debbie did not seem to be very close, and often did not sleep in the same room. Beyond the occasional slap of her ass, and calling her 'honey', John showed Debbie scant affection, and there seemed to be very little chemistry between them.

When I moved in with them, I could tell that they were not sure if they wanted a student living in their house. John saw it as extra income, to help finance his endless supply of beer; Debbie saw it as extra work for her. Regardless of this, when I arrived, they welcomed me politely, showing me where I would be staying. My bedroom, which had a small bathroom nearby, was in the basement, next to the laundry and storage room. One of the first rules Debbie imposed upon me was that I was not allowed to take a shower after 9 pm, because of the noise the water made when it ran through the pipes. I was also meant to do my own laundry in the jumble of a room next door to mine, but I got out of that by making a deal with her to wash my sheets, bedding and towels for an extra hundred dollars, instead of having to do them myself, which I was not used to. I sent my clothes to a laundry in town.

From the first moment I arrived in that house, I was enraptured with Debbie. In a powerfully arousing contrast to what I had been used to growing up, she wore tight-fitting clothing that showed off her beautiful figure licentiously. She had a freedom and ease to her movements, seemingly unaware of the riot she was causing in my pants by simply going about her day-to-day errands in what seemed to me as overtly revealing clothing.

I could not take my eyes off her: everywhere she went, everything she did; whether she was setting the table or carrying a pile of laundry down the basement stairs, I was fascinated with the way her womanly body moved around the home; her uncovered hair catching the light, the swell of her chest beneath her gaping blouse, the way her lips slowly parted when she spoke. I had a powerful sense when I first looked into Debbie's eyes that we would have sex. I saw in those eyes an urgent longing that perhaps she was not consciously even aware of at first ... an emptiness asking to be filled. I knew, in that first passing glimpse between us, when the erotic charge of our gazes met, that I had found my first American target. The hunt was on.

Debbie often liked to speak about her 'rules'. On the first day after my arrival at her home, she took me on a tour of the neighbourhood, showing me the post office, the grocery store and the laundry, where I would be sending my clothes to be washed. Neither friendly nor rude, she listed off the dictates I would have to abide by while I lived under her roof, such as: if I missed a mealtime, I would not eat; if I left a mess or took a shower after 9 pm, I would be punished; I was only half listening; I could not take my eyes off her pert, swollen breasts beneath her shirt, the buttons gaping across her cleavage that I longed to pop open; the graceful, thoughtless way she gestured with her arms. I felt myself growing aroused as I watched her speak, my erection aching as her breasts bounced beneath the thin sheath of clothing that separated them from me. I knew it would not be long before I tore that shirt open, feeling the swell of her naked breasts against my lips.

On my first morning in Debbie's house, I lingered in bed, thinking about the day before, when she had shown me around the neighbourhood. I was painfully horny, her body taking up every inch of my thoughts. I was a little unsure about whether to go upstairs for breakfast in my state, but finally, when my hunger grew too much to ignore, I got up. On my way to the kitchen, I noticed that her husband was fast asleep on the living room couch, next to three empty beer bottles on the table. I knew an opportunity when I saw one and roamed through the house until I found Debbie's bedroom. The door was ajar, and I sneaked in. The water was running, and I knew then that she was showering alone. Just the thought of the water running over her naked body made my erection rise even more.

I knocked on the door. She came out wearing a short towel. Her legs were still wet from the shower, her chest glistening; steam rising from her smooth white skin. I was dressed only in my silk boxer shorts, and even a blind woman would have been able to tell how aroused I was. Looking at me, she pulled her eyes away from me, telling me in no uncertain terms that I would not be able to stay there. She had enough problems in her life, she said; I would have to stay with another family. I pleaded in my broken English that it had been a mistake on my part, a misunderstanding. Though she knew I was lying, and that I had come into her room purposefully, she decided to give me the benefit of the doubt. I knew then that I was getting closer; slowly but surely, I was wearing her resistance down.

In the kitchen a short while later, she prepared me cornflakes while her husband snored away in the other room. I was afraid to talk to her after what had just happened, even though I really wanted her, and knew instinctively that she wanted me too. She started making polite conversation, asking me about my family back home, and whether I had a girlfriend. I explained to her about our Arabic traditions, the huge variances in our culture and upbringing, and how different America was for me. She then asked me if I was a virgin. I did not actually know what the English word meant, so, after breakfast, I looked it up in a dictionary. From my upbringing, I had learned that if a woman talks about sex, she wants it. She had confirmed what I had suspected, and my fantasies about having her naked body up against mine grew wilder.

I went to school and tried to concentrate on my studies. When I came home, I tried to do my homework, but I had become accustomed to the unlicensed pleasure the hotel porn had given me, as well as the thought of Debbie's breasts straining against her shirt … I could no longer resist putting my hands on myself. By the time I had finished, it was around 10 pm, and, without thinking, I went to take a shower. When I finished and returned to my room, Debbie was there, sitting on my bed in her nude satin nightwear.

"You're breaking the rules again," she said, looking at me fiercely. "What am I to do with you?"

I felt then that she knew I had been thinking of her as I touched myself, and that by simply coming into the room, she had communicated how she longed to be near me. When she left, I masturbated again, ejaculating purposely onto the sheets that I knew she would have to wash the following day. I wanted her to know that she aroused me, that I thought of her every time I touched myself, and every time my hot jism gushed out of my cock, that I whispered her name.

It was very hot there, and though Debbie and John owned a pool, it was too dirty to swim in. I asked her why they had not cleaned it, and she said it was too expensive, so I offered to pay for it. I was pleased to see how the new, clean pool delighted her, and shortly afterwards she invited her neighbour to join us. Sheila was not as attractive as Debbie, but I enjoyed the way she lowered her sunglasses and watched me over the top of them from the other side of the pool. But I was not interested in her; I watched from my sun lounger as Debbie dived into the cool, clear water in her barely-there bikini. I felt myself firing up as I watched the water wash over her skin.

I jumped in to cool off but took care to keep my distance while the others were watching. It was so nice to swim in the cool water beneath the sunshine, but when Debbie got out of the pool, with the rounded folds of her wet pussy on show through her bikini, I was afraid to show myself, as my erection had grown once more. I felt that she knew I was staring at her, and why. I could not dawdle for much longer in the pool without arousing comment, so I jumped out and ran into the kitchen, saying that I would get us all some drinks. Debbie called after me not to mess up her kitchen, then followed me inside. When she opened the fridge door, standing boldly there, her wet bikini clinging to her skin, I saw another opportunity. Silently, I pressed my straining erection against her ass and wrapped my arms around her stomach, aching to slip my hands underneath the wet edge of her bikini bottoms. After a moment's hesitation, she pushed me away, looking at me sternly.

"You and I are going to have to have a serious talk, young man," she said.

She was keeping me at a distance out of loyalty to her station as a wife, but I could see in her eyes that she was faltering; that it would not be much longer before I wore her defences down completely. Her eyes told me everything she would not admit.

I did not go back out to the pool after that, but listening from a nearby open window, I heard Sheila ask: "Where did that charming boy of yours get to?" Debbie started to tell her that she was having problems with me, and that she did not know how many times a day I wanked myself off.

"Meanwhile," she whispered. "I haven't had sex in five months!"

"Wow, that's a hell of a while," Sheila replied. "Personally, I would've screwed him right away if I'd had the chance!"

They laughed together dirtily, while John snoozed, half-drunk, on a sun lounger nearby. It pleased me to hear her talk about me this way; it was yet further confirmation of all I had felt by looking into her eyes.

The next day, I was called into the kitchen. John and Debbie were seated at the table, looking solemn, a tension in the air. Debbie had told John what had happened the day before in the kitchen, and she had obliged him to confront me about it. John was kind, gently explaining that I had done something I should not have, and that he needed to set some ground rules for my behaviour in the house. Debbie looked at him, shocked. It was clearly not the way she had wanted him to deal with the situation; it seemed that he was more concerned about how much extra money he could earn from the young man in his house than protecting his wife from his advances. I was very happy with this outcome; it proved to me that John was not jealous and did not care for Debbie sexually. It would be easier that way, I reasoned, for me to make my next move.

All her married life, Debbie had been dutifully playing the role of attentive wife to John and their household, and being a mother to their young daughter as she grew up. Her whole life had been oriented around her family, and since her daughter had left to go to college, all she had left to focus on was keeping the house in order, and John. But John was not satisfying her sexually, according to what she had told Sheila in the garden, and by failing to support and protect her in my presence, he had proven that he did not care for her in the way she wanted and needed.

She had gone to him out of a sense of loyalty, and a way to protect herself from my advances, which were slowly eroding the walls she had tried putting up against me; but John had not given her the protection she had longed for from him. He had all but sanctioned my behaviour: he had not fought, he had not raged, he had not kicked me out. He went on as though everything was just the same; a barely felt slap on the wrist was given, and on he went about his day, oblivious to how his wife was slipping from his grasp, right under his nose. I saw in that moment, at the breakfast table, how John's failure to stand in front of his wife had worked in my favour, and I intended to use it to my advantage.

The following morning, John left to go to work at 7 am. I usually had to leave the house at eight to get to school on time, leaving one hour in which Debbie and I were alone. After hearing him close the front door behind him, and the sound of Debbie moving around upstairs, I decided to stay in bed, knowing that the longer I dawdled and pretended to be asleep, the more likely it was that Debbie would come down to my room to wake me up, so that I would not be late for school. Lying there in my bed, biding my time, I felt like a hunter waiting for its prey to fall into the trap that had been set. After a short while, I heard her steps grow louder as she drew closer to the basement. She let herself into my room and sat beside me on the bed. Still pretending to be half-asleep, I turned over, my stiff morning erection brushing against her thigh.

"Oh my God!" she cried, standing up.

My eyes slowly peeled open. "What?" I mumbled.

"You'll be late for school," she said, looking down at me; and one area in particular.

I sat up and took her hand, hoping to draw her down onto the bed beside me, but she snatched it back.

"Don't you remember what John said yesterday? Ahmed, you need to learn to conduct yourself properly around me."

She left the room before I had a chance to answer, but I knew I had her now. I put on my shorts and went after her.

"Debbie, come on – let us talk."

"There's nothing to talk about." She sighed. "Now get dressed and go to school."

She went into her bedroom, but before she closed the door, I slipped in behind her.

"Get out!" she cried, but instead I pushed her onto the bed and fell against her, rubbing my body against hers until I came.

Afterwards, we fell silent for a while, until I spoke.

"I can only apologise, but I cannot help myself around you. Can we forget it ever happened?"

At first, she said nothing; then tears welled-up and ran down her face. "Can't you see that you're making my life more difficult?" she whispered.

The sight of her tears provoked me once more, and my cock swelled inside my shorts. I spun her over against the bed and tore her underwear down. This was the moment, the split second in which the chink in Debbie's armour had finally been found; in which I knew she would be forced to surrender to me. She had not planned it; she had tried to push back against it, but I had planted the seeds for this moment since the first day of my arrival, and no more could she suppress them.

Debbie cried, her voice breaking from the strain of her weakened resistance: "I beg you not to go any further. Please, you are stronger than me … I won't be able to stop you …"

Had she been serious, I could not have proceeded … but there was a lack of sincerity in her voice, and I could see in her eyes that these were just words; that she was finally giving in to what she truly wanted, which was for me to take her then and there. She proved this by suddenly grabbing my hard cock and pulling it inside of her, moaning loudly and trembling all over as she came instantly; coming over and over again until I too could hold back no longer, exploding inside her.

We lay together, spent, breathing raggedly in unison, steeped in a pleasurable afterglow. Then, with her underwear still clinging to her knees, she stepped gingerly to the bathroom, my juices dripping down her thighs. The sight of my silky fluids staining her skin pleased me immensely. I left the room and, smiling all the way to the basement, took a shower in my bathroom.

When we wore both clean, and all traces of what we had done were washed away, we sat together in the living room.

"It was a mistake," Debbie muttered. "I don't know how this happened …" she trailed off. "I really respect my husband, but I haven't had sex in months, and John cums so fast I'm never satisfied … and then you turn up, splashing your cum over everything and rubbing your cock up against me … you haven't made it easy for me …"

"But surely there is something missing in your relationship with John?" I suggested. "You admitted yourself that you cannot climax because he shoots his load too quickly."

"Well, yes, but life isn't perfect, I respect him, and would never leave."

"Okay," I said, playing along with her little game. "I understand." And in a way I did; but why deny herself the pleasure her body yearned for?

"If you stay here, it will happen again, so you are going to have to leave," she said with resolve in her voice.

"Debbie, I promise I will not make a move on you again," I lied; and she too knew that I was lying.

The next day, I did not go to school, and as I heard the door closing behind John, I went to her bedroom again. Without a word, I slipped her negligee off her body, waited for her to grab my pulsating member and stuff it inside her, then banged her ravenously. As I pumped inside her, she whispered: "You're hurting me!" with joy in her voice. Despite insisting that I would have to leave the house, she did not let me go, and every day, whenever we could, we fucked in every room of the house, as often as we could. Each night, I went to bed raw and aching from our frantic, stolen moments of sex, but any discomfort was offset by the ecstasy engendered by our bodies coming together, and the satisfaction of having gotten what I wanted.

During this period, Debbie softened around the house. She was no longer so forceful about her rules and was also kinder to John. Whereas before she had been snappy and irritated with him, now she was more understanding, more patient, and she seemed to serve him better as a wife. If he fell asleep on the sofa after a few beers, she did not seem to mind, as she knew it meant another stolen moment between her and me. The atmosphere between them was lighter and easier. I could see how us acting on our passions had helped them; both

Debbie and I were getting what we needed, and John's life was more easygoing because his wife no longer had the energy to nag at him about how much beer he drank.

After about a month of our trysts, Debbie sat me down at the kitchen table.

"Ahmed, you really do need to go," she began. "This is becoming a habit and I can't let it affect my marriage. I'm sure you understand."

I accepted her decision with some reluctance, packed my belongings and moved out, renting an apartment by myself. I began once again to focus on my law studies. After a month of little to no contact between us, I was struck by the desire to see Debbie again. I called her and begged her to come to my apartment. I wanted to cook for her, as a way of thanking her. After a little resistance, which thrilled me once more, she gave in. She turned up at my apartment door dressed just the way I liked, in a tight blouse that curved with her heaving breasts. She had barely closed the door behind her before I was tearing her clothes off her body. We went at it like animals all evening. And then I finally sent her home, filled up to the brim with all of me. After that, I never saw her again.

Was Debbie wrong to give in to me, and be unfaithful to her husband, with a young man she had invited into her home? Was I wrong to pursue her and throw the hospitality, and benefit of the doubt, John had shown me, back in his face? Were Debbie and I both the 'bad guys' in this story, sneaking around behind John's back while he worked to support her, or snored half-cut on the sofa? Or was I the only bad guy, obliging Debbie to give in to me against her will?

Perhaps none of us were 'bad' or 'wrong'. Perhaps Debbie was just a woman in need of some attention, to be reminded that she was desirable, and who had needs that her husband failed to meet. Perhaps I was a young man on fire with lust, which Debbie's acquiescence helped to ease. And perhaps by seducing his wife, I made John's life easier. No longer did Debbie roll her eyes or nag at him for sleeping on the sofa or drinking. No longer did he have to hear her dissatisfaction when he ejaculated after a few minutes, leaving her wanting. Perhaps I saw what each person in that household needed, and gave it to each of them, while also giving myself what I wanted.

Chapter 2 – Susan

After I finished my course at the English school, I applied for college at the same institute and got accepted. Now, I felt more confident in myself and more mature, ready for the real schooling world, and girls. The American girls, unlike the foreign ones, strapped to their rules and traditions, were so free and ready for any sexual entertainment.

Colorado was very hot in the summer, and very cold and snowy in winter. The average age of most American girls in the first year of college was eighteen. The way they dressed in the summer would not let my penis relax – tight jean shorts that accentuated the lines of their butts, and crop tops containing small and medium breasts, with nipples like bullets.

I always liked to be very discreet, and no one would ever know who I dated or had sex with. I lived in an apartment that was just a fifteen-minute drive from school, and I was totally ready to study and hit on the girls.

At the college, I could easily see the hunger for sex in the girls' eyes, whereas the boys appeared to be shy and insecure. During breaks in the canteen, I would see all kinds of female bodies and different types of beauties, and their eyes were searching for attraction all around.

Ms. Shawn, the principal of the English school, was so proud to see her students accepted at the college, and in the canteen, she often called me over, telling the teachers that I was her favourite student.

I love to have what others have and started chasing the teenage girls. My philosophy was to go and talk to my mate's girlfriend and her friends; and, eventually, they would complain about their boyfriends ... and that was the best opportunity to catch them. I was super confident that for someone like me, an 18-year-old girl would take her underwear off on the first date.

I was not planning to have a girlfriend at all. I knew it was so much more convenient to keep a few of my friends' girlfriends in my notebook and invite them to my place whenever I wanted to get laid. I was also sure that at the age of eighteen, girls spoke to each other about sex; and that they would talk about how we had sex, and the way in which we did it – and that would make other girls want me too. Oh, those girls loved getting boned by me, since there were no rules or pressure involved, as was the case with their boyfriends. Another important factor was that I was very generous with them, showering them with treats and gifts.

Susan, Ms. Shawn's daughter, was a 26-year-old history teacher. She was so hot and sexy, with blonde hair that fell a little short of her shoulders, full lips and blue eyes. She was a little chubby – I would say size 12, 163cm tall, about 34C, 29, 36 – with white skin. She always wore skimpy clothes – either a short dress or denim skirt and a black, tight tank top that made her look gorgeous. Wearing that, I could see her breasts from the front and sides, as well as the lines of her underwear.

All of us boys wanted Susan, and we used to gossip mischievously about her. We spoke about the way her eyes radiated how horny and hungry she was, and that she could never have enough sex.

Day by day, my desire for her grew, and I decided to talk to her but did not know how. One morning, I went to her mum's office, but Ms. Shawn was not there. Susan was, though, wearing a tight denim mini skirt and an open T-shirt hanging on her shoulders. She was sitting on a chair, her legs crossed.

"Can I help you?" she asked.

I looked at her naked thighs, and the flesh of her breasts on display, and smiled. "I was looking for Ms. Shawn."

"Mum should be back in ten minutes or so." She smiled back at me.

"Susan, I like you, and would like to know you more," I said boldly, cutting to the chase. "May I invite you for dinner or tea?"

"I'm too old for you," smiled Susan. "Go and find yourself a girl your age."

"I did not ask how old you are," I began. "I asked you to accept my invitation, and I did not tell you that I want to know other girls – it is you who I want to know."

"As a good talker, I don't see any problem for you dating girls, but to answer you the way you want: thank you, but sorry, I cannot."

Ms. Shawn entered the room, and I purposely hugged her, kissing her on her cheeks. "It is good to see you again, Ms Shawn," I told her.

"Oh, Ahmed is so different to my other students!" She laughed.

Susan smiled and left. When you are 20 years old, it is not easy to be taken seriously by an older woman like Susan, but I did not realise that back then.

"I like Susan a lot," I told Ms. Shawn in a serious tone.

"Everyone likes Susan." She smiled back at me. "She's so adorable!"

That afternoon, I felt so horny, so I called Cindy – a girlfriend of my friend from school – to come by my place, and after she arrived, I wasted no time in stripping her clothes from her body and banging her so hard. As I did, my mind tossed images of Susan at me, and I envisaged her lying there naked, relishing my touch and the sensation of my truncheon-like dick moving like a piston inside her.

A few days after, at lunch break, the teachers were in the school canteen. There were at least fifteen of them sitting at a table, and Susan was one of them.

"Hello, Susan," I said, walking up to the table. "I really like you and want to go out with you."

The whole table shouted, and some teachers even clapped. Susan was so embarrassed, her face flushing crimson, as all of the other teachers left the table.

"I hope you're happy with what you did," she said, looking me in the eyes.

"Honestly, yes," I replied. "As now they all know I like you."

"Sit down, Ahmed," she asked, so I obliged. "Look, I told you I'm not your age. Besides, I'm engaged, and will get married in a couple of months."

Susan then proceeded to tell me her history. Originally, her family came from Greece, arriving in America sixty years ago. She was born in the US and lived with her mum only, while her fiancé was American and worked in the US Embassy in Athens. She showed me a picture of him. He was a serious, bold-looking man, with a moustache. She said she loved him, and that they would get married in Athens. There would be no party, but they would have their honeymoon on a cruise ship.

"Ahmed, I'm flattered by your words, but I have my own life and am moving to Athens in two months' time."

"May I ask when you last saw him?" I queried, kick-starting my process.

"A couple of years ago," was her reply.

I could not believe that a sex bomb like Susan had been without sex for two whole years. It was a travesty that I aimed to reverse. "Susan, to tell you the truth, I cannot choose what I like. I am driven by my emotions and attractions, so when I say I like you, that means I truly do, and I will not change my mind. If you are engaged or married, yes maybe there will be no chance for me to be with you, but for sure I will always like you, and will be very happy if I can go out with you for dinner or a cup of tea."

"You don't take no for an answer, do you?"

"Look, I know I will end up in bed with you, and can have you whenever I want, but I want you to ask for it."

We looked at each other wordlessly for a few seconds before Susan stood up.

"I'm going to pretend you didn't say that," she said, walking off.

I do not know why I said what I did to Susan, but I guess I was driven by emotion, my lust for her, and I wanted her to have some words from me that she would never forget. I went to her mother the next day to try and explain myself.

"I do like Susan, and want to take her out," I insisted. "I am telling you this, as from my Arabic background, a woman will be controlled by her mum until she gets married."

Ms. Shawn laughed. "Tell her, Ahmed, and if she likes you, then it's her decision."

I kept trying to ask Susan out, but she refused to accept. She became easier with me, and more admiring of my words, which pleased her a lot; but the world NO was her continuous answer.

One Friday afternoon, when I was leaving school in my car, I saw Susan standing next to her blue Ford Fiesta, trying to fix it.

"What is the matter?" I asked, heading over to join her.

"I don't know – the damn thing won't start – so I need to call the Triple-A services to take it to the garage."

"Let me take you home," I offered. "The garage can collect your car for you."

"No thank you," she replied. "I'll take a taxi."

"Do not be silly," I responded, getting out of my car and opening the door to the passenger side. "Get in. It is no hassle."

"Okay, then, thanks," she said, climbing in.

I was very polite in the car, although I found it impossible not to look at her thighs touching each other, revealed by the miniskirt she was wearing.

When we reached her home, Susan's mum was not there. Susan asked if I fancied joining her for a cup of tea, which I was glad to agree to, and we went inside. The house had one floor, a living room and a kitchen, while a corridor led to three bedrooms. Sitting in the living room, Susan offered me some orange cake that she had made the day before; but before she fetched it, she went to change her clothes, returning wearing very tight black leggings and a T-shirt. She sat on the arm of the chair I was sitting on, and we had tea and orange cake.

My penis started rising, and I could not really focus on what I was saying, as my mind was centred on how horny I felt.

"With just two months to go until I leave for Greece, I need to pack, but do not have the time now, so will have to come back home at some point," she said whilst playing with her hair and then running a hand across her thigh. "Ahmed, where do your beautiful words come from? You're a great talker."

I answered as fully as I could, and we chatted for half an hour about life and what the future might hold; but that did not stop the bayonet in my pants from continuing to let me know just how much I longed to touch her.

"Well, Susan, I would like to thank you for today," I began, rising to my feet. "Can I at least have a hug before I leave?"

She smiled and hugged me, her breasts pressing against my chest, which made my throbbing member rise even more, hitting her stomach. Silently hugging and feeling each other, I lowered my hand and slid it across her crotch to discover she had no underwear on.

"Which is your room?" I whispered.

"At the end of the corridor, to the right," she whispered back.

Hugging Susan and walking her to her room, she was silently accepting my advances. Sitting her down on her bed, I stepped back and pulled my jeans and underwear down at the same time. My cock rose up so big, like an old seventeenth-century key, and I proceeded to pull her leggings down to her knees, opened her legs and slid it all the way into her. She was so wet and horny, and moaned before climaxing with a lengthy groan. The feeling of her wet pussy enveloping my trouser snake was a joy, but then, all of a sudden, we heard her mum parking up outside.

"Oh, God, it's my mum!" Susan exclaimed. "Get dressed – quickly! – before she comes in."

I did as she asked, throwing my clothes back on, then followed Susan into the living room, where a minute or so later, we were joined by Ms. Shawn, who greeted me with a smile. Susan explained why I was there, and I had another piece of cake, then left.

Standing under the shower in my apartment, my emotions seesawed between pleasure and dissatisfaction. I felt like a lion who had caught his prey but had not had the chance to eat it. I wanted to go back to her so badly, knowing Susan and I had unfinished business. Then, around 11 pm, she called me:

"Ahmed, I need to be sure of two things. Firstly, that you'll be a good boy and keep what happened between us secret. Secondly, I'm not the sort of woman to go to bed with younger men or students, and I don't know how that happened; but I haven't been touched in, oh, I don't know – too long – and to be honest, I've missed sex. So, I gave myself to you, because that's what my body willed me to do."

"Do not worry," I tried to reassure her. "I understand you have principles, and I am not about to undermine them. But be sure that I want to see you again."

"Okay, you can come at half-eleven," she shot back at me without hesitation. "But don't come before, because I don't want to wake my mum up, or for her to know that you've been here. And when you arrive, come with a copy of the Koran, your holy book."

At 11.28, I was at the door, waiting. Susan opened the door five minutes later, wearing a white nightie, no bra and white underwear. All but dragging me to her room, she laid me down on her bed.

"Ahmed, I want to fuck you. You said you wanted me to ask for it, so now I am."

I pressed Susan's lips against mine as she touched her breast, then, with my jeans still on, traced my penis over her body.

"I am sorry for the afternoon sex," I said, barely able to think amid my delirium. "So now, in return, I shall let you take me whichever way you want."

"Don't move," was her instruction, before she started unbuckling my belt and pulling my jeans down.

When she saw my angry dick rising, she moaned and started sucking it. I loved how she took control of the situation, greedily sucking so hard, and taking so much of it in her mouth that I wondered if she was trying to swallow it whole. She kissed my nipples and neck, then wrapped her palm around my tool and drove it into her twat. Riding me like a rodeo, her pussy was soaking wet, showering my dick, and she did not take too long to cum. She was not looking at me when we shagged, but after she came, she stared right at me and whispered: "You drive me crazy, and I love fucking you, Ahmed – you really fill me in right!"

She did not pull my penis out, floating like a dhow in the sea, while smiling with naughtiness and pleasure. Turning her over onto her back, I started giving her slow, deep strokes. Her pussy was hot, wet and tight and, before too long, she effortlessly rolled onto her belly, positioning herself perfectly so that I could take her doggie style. Holding my penis, I guided it back into her minge and started taking her from behind. The waves of her butt moving back and forth, hitting my tummy, drove me crazy, and she begged me to cum inside her ... and, in no time, I exploded, filling her with my juices.

We laid on her bed for a few moments, but a couple of minutes later Susan landed back in reality.

"Ahmed, I hate you. How could I do it? I really love my fiancé ... what made me do it?"

"Susan, I never thought you would have sex with me. You acted how you felt and did what you needed. Did you not like it?"

"You don't ask a woman if she liked it – I just came three times!"

I wanted to stay overnight, to feel her again, but she insisted I leave, so I did as she asked. A 26-year-old woman, engaged to a very successful man working for the Foreign Ministry, who was getting married in two months' time, and had plans in place for her future life, including having children, being supported by her husband, had fallen into a trap laid by a 20-year-old boy.

From another perspective, a woman so hot and horny had not seen her man for two years, and maybe he was even talking to her sexually on the phone, firing her up even more. She would have seen teenagers at college, with sexual romance all around, and I had no doubt that her innate sexual needs were dominating her brain; so the second she felt my big, hard penis rubbing against her tummy, she surrendered to her natural demands and sexual desires. The only thing she could or would have thought of was to have that big dick filling her, to release all the frustration that had built up. There was not a chance that her brain had anything in it except that penis, and that is why she took it.

Susan would fly out to her husband with her own little secret, more relaxed and in a better frame of mind, prepared for her future life; and I was sure that she learnt something positive to take with her, aware of how important her sexuality was to her, and how best she might satisfy it.

Chapter 3 – Jenny

I liked moving from town to town, never staying in one place. Westminster was a small town between Denver and Boulder, with all the basic services, but nothing fancy. It was only ten minutes' drive from Denver, which made it the ultimate place for me to be able to focus on my studies; and, moreover, I could discreetly bring my flames in.

I rented a one-bedroom apartment in a three-storey building. Each floor had two apartments, but no elevator, there were no facilities, like a gym or tennis court, but it was safe and clean. I was always very discreet about my private life, and never gave anyone the chance to know who I was with or who I was dating. I was normally careful about making friends with my neighbours, and so ensured I was very quiet going in and out, minding my own business in the compound.

One day, I noticed three people living on the ground floor – two men and a girl. I was not sure about the relationship between them but wondered why they were sharing a one-bedroom apartment.

One of them was called Jenny, a smiley girl in her twenties, with red curly hair, blue eyes, healthy round breasts and a lifted butt. I could tell that it was one of those butts that invites a doggie style position, and we walked past each other on many occasions. David was about 22 years old, very tall at around 191cm, handsome, short hair, not muscly, but not fat, extremely polite and well-mannered. One was forced to respect him the second one saw him.

Rob was same age as David, and always wore a hat. A short guy at maybe 160cm, he had a look in his eyes that would not allow you to trust him. The first month I was there, we all smiled when passing each other on a walkway, but did not engage in conversation.

David and Rob were out most of the time, but without Jenny. It was later that I found out that Jenny was married to David, who worked at a Red Lobster diner. Rob was David's best childhood friend, and they both worked on a cruise ship before. Rob was in his last year of university, but Jenny did not work, or study – she could not afford it but, moreover, she was not interested. She seemed to be happy being David's wife, the man she loved and wanted to have three kids with, and one day move to Missouri, Illinois, and live on a ranch.

In the meantime, I enrolled in five classes, one of which was American History, which I thoroughly enjoyed. My life was very organised. I went to university in the morning, returned home, cooked for a couple of hours, took a nap, studied for a while, then did two hundred push-up and sit-ups before going to sleep.

At that time, I was relieving my sexual needs with a girl called Monica, who worked in an Arabic restaurant. She was living with her mum and loved to chat to me and talk about her dreams, and what she could be in the future. She would visit me once a week, every Tuesday.

One day, I saw Jenny and David unloading their groceries from their car and offered to help them. Straight after, I invited them to my apartment for dinner, and this is how our friendship began.

I was totally mesmerised by Jenny's beauty and energy. All of my principles collapse when faced by beauty and, in my mind, there was only one task and desire – I simply had to have her. I had so many questions in my head, though, the most prominent of which was: how would I conquer her when she was so attached to David? Even though I was confident about my abilities, he was more handsome than me, plus he was her loving husband. Whilst plotting my plan to seduce her, I had to settle for images of Jenny's beautiful body when having sex with Monica.

Jenny and I became close friends very quickly, and her visits became more frequent. She loved my tea and was helping me to cook so that she could learn how to do it herself. David knew and liked the fact that Jenny was not wasting time, sitting at home, bored.

She would come to my apartment without knocking, whereas David was the opposite – he would never enter without knocking. We spent a lot of time together playing cards and video games, and my desire for Jenny was growing, as she was around me every day, and I would keep staring at her bum and breasts all the time. Jenny could see in my eyes that I wanted her so badly. She showed up at my house daily, except for Tuesdays, which she avoided, knowing that was when I had company – Monica's company. Since they needed some extra cash, Jenny started cleaning my apartment, which was a win-win situation for both of us – Jenny got an extra

$200 a month, and I would be closer to her. One day, she asked me:

"Ahmed, who's the girl who comes every Tuesday to see you? We all wait for her every week and bet whether she'll show up."

"Her name is Monica," I began answering, sure that she posed the question with an ulterior motive in mind. "She has problems with her mum, and I am simply trying to help her."

"Oh, I'm sure you're helping her in many ways!" laughed Jenny.

One night, when three of us were together, David talked about an Italian restaurant that he liked the look of, but never went to, as it was too expensive, so I decided to take them there. The restaurant was called Coliseum, located in Evans Boulevard in Denver. One day before we went, David apologised that he would have to work that night. That did not make Jenny happy, but David gave her the green light for us to go without him, to which she agreed.

The next morning, I gave Jenny $50 and asked her to visit a beauty salon to pamper herself and make herself even more beautiful. At 6.30 pm, we took my car and I let Jenny drive. She looked like a mature woman with her make-up on and a lovely hairstyle. She wore her curly hair loose, but it was parted from the middle and gathered from the back. She wore a sleeveless black dress, which stopped a little above her knees, emphasising all her curves. The restaurant was not very busy, with only a few tables taken. When we were going through the menu, I posed a question to her:

"Jenny, I want us to play a game, but only if you promise that whatever we talk about will remain in the restaurant and will not affect our friendship. I also ask that we be honest with each other."

Jenny's expression immediately morphed into one of excitement and curiosity. "Why not?" she responded, an understated smile playing across her lips.

We both ordered a steak, but Jenny could barely eat, so keen was she to start the game. And so I began, as requested, asking: "Who is Rob?"

"He's a jerk and I don't like him. He's a friend of David's, but he's taking advantage of him. David's too kind and generous sometimes, but we need the extra income from his rent. The thing is, having Rob there interferes with our personal life, and we have next to no privacy."

"Okay, now your turn," I said.

Jenny paused for a few moments before asking: "Will your parents choose your future wife for you?"

"No, but they will recommend one, and I certainly will not speak to her before the marriage."

Jenny looked at me with her lips agape, surprise etched onto her face.

"I know how strange that might sound, but this is our Arabic tradition, and we need to follow it. My turn now – when was the last time you had sex?"

Another pause. I could clearly see in her eyes that she was pondering what to say, which meant she would lie.

"No lying." I reminded her. "A deal is a deal."

"Two months ago," she finally answered.

I could tell that she was telling the truth, and was amazed, having assumed she was having sex every other day. We exchanged a few more questions and answers, and then agreed to a final round.

"What are the three things on your wish list?" I asked.

"First, having my privacy with David," she began. "Second, buy some clothes and shoes for summer. Third, a watch for me and David. And yours?"

"Well, first, I will make your second and third wish come true. Second, that we can play this game anytime, provided we are honest. And third, kissing you tonight." As I posed my third wish, I saw so many things in Jenny's eyes:

1. Who did I think I was, daring to say that?
2. It was evident that she desperately missed the passion and desire that sex provided.
3. She was flattered that I explicitly said I wanted her.
4. I could see the emotional battle inside of her between resistance and desire.

Saying nothing in response, Jenny made her way to the toilet and, a couple of minutes later, I followed her. My heart was beating super-fast, and my adrenaline was rising as I pushed the door to the ladies' room open, to see her standing alone by the washbasin.

"I am sorry, but it has to be tonight," I declared, kissing her on the lips.

She kissed me back, but only for a few seconds, before gently pushing me away. With the horniest eyes I've ever seen, she looked at me and said: "You've got your wish now. Don't ever try this again!"

Driving home, I was careful not to mention my desire for her. I spoke to her about the sandy desert and clear night skies back home, keeping the conversation light and airy. When we got home, David was still not there. We knew he would not be home for another hour or so, so Jenny came up with me and we played chess.

In both our minds, we kept replaying our restaurant game. Of course, I knew that it was invented for a specific purpose – simply to penetrate Jenny's brain, reawakening her deeply hidden passions and sexual desire. For the next few days, we acted as we did before, but our eyes were saying different things and challenging our patience.

I could still recall the flavour of our first kiss on my lips, and I could not get over it. What made it so much harder was that Jenny was hanging around my apartment most of the time, making me want her even more. I did not want to scare her and make a silly move; I just wanted her to enjoy it and inflate her ego by being wanted so much. In my mind, I knew by now that she was thinking of me while touching herself.

It was Thursday when David said he had a double shift over the weekend and would not be able to hang out with us, to which I answered that I would be taking Jenny out shopping and that we would get a few things for him too. Jenny and I decided to go to the mall around 10 am, and that afterwards we would watch a movie, cook, and then play chess and other games.

On the way to the mall, I asked: "Jenny, are you upset about our kiss?"

"I'm not sure who I should be upset with, or whether I should be upset at all."

"Remember my second wish: that we play my game any time we want."

"I can take part, Ahmed," she answered. "But it won't get you anywhere."

"Okay, deal. So, here goes: does David have a problem having sex with you?"

"Yes."

"Do you touch yourself every day?"

"Yes."

"Do you think about me having sex with Monica the minute she arrives?"

"Yes."

"Have you ever thought of me and Monica when you touched yourself?"

"Yes."

"Did you touch yourself the night we had dinner?"

"Yes."

"Can you tell and see that I want you?"

"Yes."

"Do you like the fact that I want you?"

"Yes."

"Did you like the kiss between us?"

"Yes, but that doesn't mean I'll do it again."

When we reached the mall, we finished our game. At the mall, we got two shirts and two ties for David. For Jenny, we got an M. Kors watch and, for David, an Armani one. I also bought her two pairs of Armani shoes and Nike trainers. Then we went to buy some clothes for her.

"Jenny, you can have whatever you like, but you need to try it on first. Why not start with some underwear?"

"I can't," she said. "My husband won't be happy about it, and I just want a couple of summer dresses."

She chose two short dresses – one red and one green, both with a flowery pattern, cut to expose her breasts, and with zips that went all the way from the neck to the butt. The dresses were so short that if she bent down slightly, her butt lines were exposed.

In the changing room, Jenny asked a sales assistant to assist her with one of the dresses, but I was faster and jumped straight in to help. Her entire back was open, I could see her white underwear, and I quickly pulled the zip up, saying: "I am better at unzipping," while kissing her back.

"Stop teasing me." She sighed, which to me meant stop joking around. The hint of a smile surfaced. "But you can help me zip the other dress up."

"I'm not joking with you," I answered whilst zipping her next dress up.

I was only too happy to oblige, she came out looking super sexy and very pretty, and she was very happy with her choice. We both agreed that the dresses looked great on her, I paid for them, and we drove back home. On the way there, she asked me if I knew what teasing meant, and I said yes – it was when you joked with somebody. Jenny then explained that it had another meaning – making somebody want you, but not allowing them to have you. It was then that I realised she wanted me and felt sure that any teasing would be short-lived; pretending not to notice as she looked me over, sizing me up.

Jenny recommended that we rent Bambi, so that we could watch it while cooking later, which of course we did. I told her:

"Today is your day, and I will treat you like a princess. You should just relax, and I will do everything for you – the cooking, the serving, and even the feeding."

We reached home, went to my apartment, and I started cooking. I told Jenny to relax in the meantime and got her a T-shirt and shorts to change into. Jenny suggested that she return to her apartment to change, but I told her it was not a good idea, as an already sceptical Rob would get more suspicious, so she stayed. At some point she suggested she should help, so I asked her to slice some vegetables for salad.

"How do you want them sliced?" she asked.

I stood behind her and, holding her hand, started slicing a cucumber. My penis started rising up, hitting Jenny's butt. She released herself and headed straight to the door.

"I think it's best I leave," she declared.

I ran after her and begged her to stay.

"No more kisses!" she said firmly.

"No more kisses," I echoed, while starting to kiss her regardless. I looked her deep in the eye, requesting: "Say it again."

"No more kisses," she repeated. "No more, no more!" she went on, while we continued to kiss each other passionately.

I pulled Jenny down onto the floor and started peeling her T-shirt off, kissing her beautiful breasts. "No more, no more," I repeated like a mantra until reaching her shorts. "No more, no more," I continued, kissing her underwear, then licking and nibbling her drenched pussy.

Pulling her underwear to one side, I slid my hard penis inside her. She was on top of me, rocking slowly at first, before upping the pace to the point that she rode me furiously, losing control until she came. I then took her to my bed and fucked her doggie style until I came. I woke up about an hour later; kissed Jenny's back and gave her a towel to take a shower. I took a shower myself and finished preparing the food.

When she came out, I kissed her on the lips, and she kissed me back.

"That was wrong," she said.

"It felt right, but a wrong thing to do. So, Jenny, I promise not to try and take you again. We should act like adults and move on – let us forget about it."

We had our dinner and watched Bambi. I fell asleep again, and when I opened my eyes, Jenny was still there but wearing her own clothes, which meant she got changed at home in the meantime.

Around 10 pm, David came home from his shift, and we gave him his gifts, which made him very happy. Jenny also showed him her shopping, to which David commented that there was no surprise she was looking so happy. They both thanked me and left, as David had to be up early for work again.

The next morning, I awoke with one thing on my mind – Jenny's body, and the manner in which it moved when having sex with me. I kept staring through the window, checking if and when David left for work. Finally, I spotted him driving off, at which point I could hear my heart beating louder and faster. All I wanted was to get to Jenny and take her to bed again.

After five minutes, I knocked on her door and she opened it, wearing a light-yellow bathrobe.

"Ahmed, what do you want?" she asked.

I could not spit a word out, but it was very clear to both of us what I really wanted.

"We can't keep doing this," she said.

"You are right – we sure cannot," I replied, taking her hand in mine and leading her towards her room. "Come with me, I want to tell you something."

"No no," she said, with a distinct lack of conviction in her voice.

"Do not worry, I will not do anything," I lied. As soon as we entered her room, I pushed her onto the bed and opened her robe, revealing her beautiful, naked body. I took my hard, throbbing penis out, lifted Jenny's legs up with one hand and started screwing her, saying: "I promised I would not make love to you again."

Jenny was loving it and kept saying: "Promise me: no more!"

At that moment, I felt she was mine, and she gave me the impression that she loved being mine; and although she kept saying no, her hands pushed my butt, driving me deeper into her. Orgasming, she groaned with pleasure, inviting me to do the same: "Ahmed, I beg of you: cum inside me!"

I gave her a few deeper strokes and felt my penis fully immersed in her body. And then I could hold out no longer: I kept coming inside of her, then lay on top of her, with my penis still buried in her snatch, prolonging our insane pleasure.

Jenny looked at me and said: "You are going to do this to me again!"

I kissed her and whispered into her ear: "You can have me any time you want."

Jenny slipped, and I believed she did not plan to cheat on David. As much as she enjoyed my admiration and attention, she was confident of being able to resist my advances, and her own desire.

Despite the mundaneness of her daily routine, she was a very positive, good woman who knew what she wanted from life, and what she wanted to achieve with David. She was certain that, eventually, they would overcome their sexual problems and be happy together.

It was a challenge to penetrate Jenny's mind and soul, but I took my time and skilfully planted the seeds of my desire in her. I kept expressing my admiration with my eyes, my body language, complements, and my questions game to make her feel wanted and needed.

It took me a while, but she finally conceded defeat to her resistance, and I was sure she loved what she did with me. She was very passionate, filled with lust and desire, and I could feel how hungry she was for amazing sex … and I felt it had been far too long since she last had that. Despite her internal battle with her emotions and pride, and reiterating that she did not want me to continue, her eyes and body were begging for me not to stop.

Jenny was desperate for the right sex, and I gave it to her. We kept at it for another two months, almost every day, until her sexual needs and hunger were fulfilled. This is when she was finally able to wake up from her lustful daydream and start to revisit her reality, and the life she had planned with David. I was just a station in Jenny's train of life and felt sure she would never forget the experience, had learnt a lot from it, and moved on to a happier life with her husband. As far as I was concerned, she was a wonderful station in my train of life too.

Chapter 4 – Maha

Not every lion can hunt, but those who can really know how to target weak prey. A flight from the USA to Emirates lasted around twenty-eight hours in the '80s, so we often took a short break in a country in-between, which more often than not saw us in London, a city that was pretty much sandwiched between the two.

In 1989, I returned home to visit my family in the summer. On the way back, I stopped over in London for a few days, staying in the Gloucester Hotel in Kensington, a four-star establishment with a casino attached to it. At the reception, while I was checking in, a married couple from Saudi were doing the same. The wife was dressed in a white wedding dress and looked very pretty and sexy. The groom was wearing a smart black suit.

Normally, you do not talk to an Arabic man whilst he is with his wife. Nevertheless, I politely congratulated him on his marriage, and he responded very generously, introducing himself to me:

"Hello, I am Khalil, and this is my wife, Maha. We got married yesterday but have not met yet… if you know what I am talking about."

He said that with a smile on his face, whilst looking at Maha. Of course, that meant they had yet to have sex. Maha looked very shy, which made her even sexier. She was about 162cm, 62kg, with a 36-28-38-inch figure. In my head, I thought of her: 'A perfect prey ready to be tasted – what more could an expert lion wish for?' – although in my mind I was certain there was no chance of me touching Maha, or even getting close to her. Saudi is more restricted than Emirates, so if you think of sex sixteen times a day in Emirates, they think about it a hundred times a day in Saudi. I politely congratulated them again, took my room key and headed to the elevator, purposely waiting for them to join me there, so that I would know their floor number. In the elevator, I pressed the button for the fifth floor, and Khalil said: "Same floor, my friend." Maha stared at the ground, and never once looked into my eyes.

My room number was 536; theirs was 538. Before entering our rooms, Khalil asked me about the casino and bar in the hotel. I told him he had better go to the casino, where he could gamble while having a drink, and we entered our respective rooms. Closing the door to mine, I immediately put my ear to the connecting door between our rooms, trying to hear what I expected to be going on – i.e. them having sex, and screaming ... but, unfortunately, there was nothing to hear.

I called laundry services to iron my clothes and went out for a stroll. It was about 6 pm in London. Around nine, I changed my clothes and headed to the casino, hoping to see my neighbours there. The minute I stepped through its doors, Khalil spotted me, meandering my way to hug me with a full glass of whiskey in his hand, out of his mind on drink.

"You see how alone I am without my wife?" he slurred. "Ahmed, I love you so much, my friend – you are the best kind of man this world can offer!"

I was surprised by what he was saying, because we had never met before, yet he was all over me.

"I am afraid I have to leave," I told him, keen to untangle myself from his drunken embrace.

Khalil looked at me and said: "Do not make a mistake with your room number!"

Heading out for another stroll, I returned to the casino at 12 am, hoping not to find him there, but he was still around and welcomed me passionately:

"Ah, Ahmed, you returned my brother!" he chuckled, his breath soaked in alcohol.

Personally, I never drink and hate to be around intoxicated people. "How long have you been here?" I asked.

"Right after I got into my room!" he declared rather boastfully.

"But what about your wife? Should you not be with her?"

"Listen, she will go nowhere. I will screw her anytime I want, but alcohol I cannot find any time I want."

He was totally shitfaced, falling over, and badly needed some sleep. I insisted I take him to his room, but when we got there, he did not have his card; so I knocked on the door and, from the other side of it, in a soft voice, I heard Maha's voice:

"Who is it?"

"I am the man from next door. Your husband is with me, and he needs help."

She opened the door, wearing pale green buttoned pyjamas. Her pants were filled with her 38-inch hips, while her top strained under the weight of her heavy boobs. Her hair was not covered, hanging mid-length between her hips. Khalil was totally lost, so I helped him to bed, and he fell asleep.

I politely made my way out of the room and, as I did, out of the corner of my eye, I noticed that the TV was on, with a porn movie playing. I went back to my room and stuck my ear to the connecting door, trying to hear it but, again, there was nothing to listen to. About fifteen minutes later, the phone in my room rang, and it was Khalil's wife. She was very polite, thanking me for my help and slowly opening up, talking about herself.

Living under very strict rules, she could not leave the room without Khalil who, when not drunk or asleep, wasted time watching television. I told her there was a lot to see in London, and that I would invite them both for lunch. I sensed dissatisfaction in Maha, who I was sure wanted me to pay her compliments on how hot and sexy she was, but I did not do this.

The next morning, around 11 am, I knocked at their door. A half-asleep Khalil answered, inviting me in. I politely refused, telling him that I would like him and his wife to join me for lunch at 3 pm. He accepted, and we agreed that we would leave together from our rooms. At 2.30 pm, Maha called my room again and, crying heavily, shouted that she did not know what to do.

I hung up and went knocking on her door. When she opened, I found her crying, and she invited me in. Wearing a white silk shirt and jeans, she sat down. The way her butt filled her jeans, the tears in her eyes, and my being alone with her made me want to stick my dick in her without a second's delay.

"What is wrong?" I asked.

"Khalil has been in the bar since twelve," she whimpered, rising to her feet as my wang rose in my pants. "He is drunk again and does not want to go anywhere."

I edged closer to her and hugged her, trying to calm her down; but as I did, my dick hit her tummy. Her reaction was firm and clear – she pushed me away, saying: "No, I am not that type of girl."

She even looked a little scared, and asked me to leave, which, of course, I did. Around ten minutes later, she called to apologise for her reaction, explaining that she was still a virgin and had yet to be touched. I told her that I totally understood and explained that hugging is very normal in the USA, where I was studying.

Slowly she grew more relaxed, and I convinced her to go out for a walk, saying that upon our return, we would find Khalil and take him to lunch. After twenty minutes of walking, we returned to the hotel and found Khalil, who insisted we join him for a drink. An Arabic man will never ask his wife to drink next to another man unless he is totally drunk. It could not have been more obvious that Maha felt extremely embarrassed and disappointed, so she returned to their room. I left Khalil to it and followed her up to their room, the door to which she was standing by, in tears.

I reached out to her and hugged her again, but this time she did not complain, so I looked into her eyes and whispered: "Come to my room." We entered it without a word, and I pushed her onto my bed, saying: "You are a bad girl, Maha! You watch a lot of porn, and deserve to be fucked, just like one of those bad girls."

Maha kept repeating one sentence: "I swear, I am not like that!"

I unzipped her jeans and, as I started pulling them down, noticed her hips fighting to find a way out of them; then lifted her butt to make it easier for me. She was shaking, insisting: "Ahmed, I am not like that!"

"I will lick your nipples," I told her as my stiff member slammed against her thighs. "And now your hungry pussy."

When my big, hard, angry dick was ready for her first penetration, she mumbled: "Be gentle, please."

Sliding just the tip of my wang in, she moaned and surrendered to me totally. Now, I knew I was in control, and I knew she loved it. I eased a little more inside her, and she moaned again, biting her lips.

"Maha, I will take it out," I threatened.

"Please do not!" she shot back at me. "Put a little more of it in …"

Not a man to refuse a request of that nature, I gradually eased the rest of my big, fat sausage in. She had no sexual experience but had watched a lot of porn; and the manner in which she moved her body made me sure that she had taken her lead from the girls in those films; that she wanted to be just like them. My very slow, lengthy strokes drove her crazy, and she kept screaming: "I will cum! I will cum! I will cum! Oh, I am! I am!"

Her joyous exclamations made me cum too, my love paste flying out of my cock like a supersonic train going at full pelt. Lying there, saying nothing to each other for several minutes, Maha stood up, put her clothes on and, after giving me a mischievous smile, left for her room. Craven for sex, and loaded with porn movie fantasies, I truly think I found the perfect prey. She made no contact with me again until 12 am, when she called to politely ask if I could check on her husband, acting as if nothing had happened between us.

I said sure, found Khalil in the casino, and persuaded him to return to his room. Drunk again, he could barely stand, and it was a hell of a job getting him there. When I knocked on the door, Maha opened up wearing a baby doll nightie, her thighs and breasts exposed. Dragging a murmuring, incoherent Khalil to bed, I went to the connecting door and quickly unlocked it. She thanked me, and I told her I would return in a little while to ensure Khalil was okay, using the connecting door to do so.

When I returned, he was sleeping deeply, while Maha was watching porn, with the actors screwing doggie style. Neither of us said a word as we continued to watch for a few seconds, until I seized her by the hand and led her to my room, via the connecting door, which I closed behind us. Without saying anything, Maha laid on her tummy, lifting her ass up, perfectly positioning herself to be taken from behind. Pulling her panties aside, I touched her pussy, which was hot, wet and, for sure, hungry again, wishing to feast on my trouser snake. I stroked her hips with it, and said: "Sorry, Maha, I only fuck bad girls, and you said you are not one of them ..."

With a voice saturated with lust, she said: "No – I am so bad, please take me!"

"No, Maha, no – I am afraid I might hurt you."

"Ahmed, I need you to do it to me. Fuck me as hard as you desire. And if you choose to punish me first, then you must. I do not want you to spank me, but if you must, you must."

I took this as my invitation to do exactly that, as she lifted her butt even higher, burying her face in a pillow. Bringing my palm down on one cheek, then another, she gasped as it stung her flesh; and I continued to spank her while screwing her, plunging my love truncheon into her hot pussy, which leaked fluid onto her thighs. Replicating the moves she would have seen in the porn films, the thought of her man being just a few feet away made me even harder, and want her even more.

Maha kept cumming, and begged me not to cum inside her, so I asked her to turn around and, when I was ready to spurt, I pulled my dick out to spray a trail of jism from her tummy to her throat. Again, saying nothing, she grabbed a tissue to clean herself with, put her knickers back on then left to return to her room.

I was leaving the next day on an early flight and, when I told her, she asked to bid farewell to me in my shower. I do not know if it made me a good or bad person, but the sound of Maha, the look of her pussy under the running water and knowing that her husband was next door and she was cheating on him made me even a stronger hunter, more dominating of her kingdom.

I never saw Maha again, and do not know why a young lady who had just got married, ready for a beautiful life of loyalty to her husband, would do something like that, unless he really forced her into that situation by depriving her of sexual pleasure; but I knew how to strike at the right time. I certainly helped Maha with her feelings at that moment, and I gave her what she wanted at that point in her life. In my world, she was not a cheater; merely a woman who followed her true feelings, enjoyed herself and learned to appreciate the importance of responding to her body's needs.

Chapter 5 – Christie and Noora

In college, most Arab students had problems with algebra, whereas I found it so easy and fun, so I used to teach a lot of them. Ibrahim – a student from Kuwait who I called Ibra – was super rich and very shy. He was your typical Arabic person, not taking care of his body and not particularly stylish.

About 165cm tall and weighing 95kg, he drove a Porsche and lived in Cherry Creek, the most expensive area in Denver. I taught him algebra, and he offered to pay me for it, but I did not accept it. Ibrahim really liked me and my ways, and warmed to my sense of humour. I also liked him a lot. He was a very nice person who was polite and generous but, unfortunately, he was a typical Arabic student in that he had a big problem when it came to alcohol – namely, that he liked too much of it. As already stated, I do not drink at all, but I would not let it put me off him, as I valued his company. Visiting him at his house, I noticed he had a different girlfriend every time … until realising they were prostitutes. I also noticed that when they went to his room, the sex between them lasted a matter of seconds.

With time, he confided in me, explaining that he had a big problem: ejaculating too quickly before he even touched a woman. He was drunk and crying, and so I told him we should talk about it when he sobered up.

The next morning, I called him and invited him to join me for lunch. Ibrahim opened up, giving me a rundown of his life, from A to Z – he had huge wealth, was his parents' only son, with five sisters, one of them studying in Boulder, Colorado, and his dad was in his seventies. He was also in love with a girl called Christie, who worked in a jewellery store, and despite being with a lot of women, he had never had sex with any of them, including Christie. He believed she loved him for his personal attributes, not his money, which is why he was planning to marry her. He also believed she would help cure him of his premature ejaculation.

"Does your family know about your problem?" I asked.

"Yes, my sister, Noora," he answered.

"Does she know Christie?"

"Yes, they know each other."

"How come I never see your sister?" I asked.

"Oh, I am sure you will in time. She has not had much luck in her life. Her husband died in a car accident, here in Denver, when his car skidded in the snow, and he crashed."

"Ibrahim," I began in a strong voice. "You must see a doctor. This is not a joke, it is a very serious matter, and I believe you must change your style, and take care of your body. Firstly, you must see a doctor. Secondly, you must join a gym. And thirdly, we have to kit you out with a new wardrobe and have you looking handsome and stylish, in good clothes."

He accepted it right away, so we found a gym to join. Ibrahim insisted he pay for me, so I let him. The following day, we went to Neiman Marcus, to shop for him, before moving on to see a doctor. To begin with, he was alone with a female doctor, but he asked me to join them. The advice I heard her impart was not to force the issue and to try not to let women take their clothes off before any contact between them. The doctor insisted he take no form of medication for four weeks, to have no sexual contact in that time, and for them to meet again the following month. As we left the clinic, Ibrahim told me he thought the doctor was right, as he had been in the habit of hiring a hooker each day to try and solve his issue; and that he really loved Christie and wanted things to work out with her.

It was summer in Colorado, and I decided to visit my family overseas for three weeks. Upon my return, I called Ibra. He was happy to know I was back, inviting me for dinner at his house. Arriving there, I saw a red Ferrari parked next to his Porsche and, after being invited in, he introduced me to his sister, Noora. A very polite lady, 27 years old, she was moderate in her presentation; though I could tell she was rich by the quality of the stylish, understated jewellery she wore. She had short dark hair, brown eyes, full lips that had clearly been artificially inflated, and stood at around 168cm, with a 42-28-38 body shape.

As we sat to eat, it was clear that we would discuss family issues. Both Ibra and Noora drank, but she was much more considered in her intake and, four years older than her brother, had the confidence to boss the table. Ibra ignored the advice given by the doctor, continuing to hire hookers while deciding against going to the gym.

"Ahmed, Ibra speaks so highly of you that I would like to hear your advice," said Noora.

"Well, I do not want to pin any blame on him, but I do want to help. However, before I talk to somebody, I need to know him or her, so please tell me about yourself."

We all moved to the living room, and they both had alcohol.

"Yes, my brother told me how good you are, but now I can also see how dangerous you are, Ahmed." She smiled seductively, sipped from her glass, then continued. "So, I will tell you this: I studied for a master's in philosophy, I am the fourth child in the family, and I got married to my cousin a couple of years ago. But he died in a car accident and, thankfully, we do not have any children, as it would have been so hard on them, as well as me."

"Thank you, Noora," I said, chewing gum that had lost its flavour. "I can be dangerous, but in a good way, and have a method of evaluating life that I do not expect others to follow."

Ibrahim was on his third glass of whiskey when, slurring, he declared: "Noora, I told you he was something else – right?!"

"Ibrahim has more than just his sexual problems to deal with, so you and I – and Christie, if you think she is good for him – all must work together to help him. Have you met Christie?"

"Not yet," I answered.

"Then I think you should judge her for yourself. I really like her a lot, and think she is good for Ibra."

It was a Friday night, and we all agreed to go out for lunch the following Sunday. Christie would come along too, it was decided; and I would meet her for the first time the following day in the mall she worked in. Ibra was so drunk that I excused myself and headed home.

The next day, I visited the mall as planned. There, in a general store called GINI, selling designer jewellery, stood Christie, who I recognised from the photo Ibra showed me. She wore jeans that were so tight they may as well have been a second skin, coupled with a denim shirt open to the middle, relieving her bra and showing what she had. I put her vital statistics at around 170cm, 36b-26-34, and around 20 to 21 years old, with tanned skin and long black, permed hair.

Honestly, I could say nothing of how attractive she was, and I left the shop right away, returning around five minutes later; then repeated the process, at which point Christie approached me.

"Are you okay? Is there anything I can help you with?"

"Hello, I am looking to buy a ring," I said.

"Who are you buying the ring for?" she asked.

"For my father," I replied. "Can I share something with you? My dad is a psychiatrist, who taught me how to read people from their eyes."

"Well, that is interesting, I must say. And your name is?"

"Ahmed. Often, my guesses are right, so allow me to consider you." I ran a hand across my mouth, allowing my forehead to crease in fake contemplation. "I think you are a girl who was born in November, and you look more Sagittarius than Scorpio."

"Wow – amazing!" she shrieked with excitement.

"Let me tell you something else," I went on. "You look like a girl who would date a guy from the Middle East."

"From which country?" Christie asked, intrigued.

"Oh, I am not that good." I smiled, offering her my number.

"I am afraid I have a boyfriend who is really good to me," she said. "And I think we are going to get married."

It was not hard for me to notice Christie's hungry eye for sex, and knowing that I would see her the next day made her even more desirable.

I ended up buying a beautiful crest ring with an emerald centre stone, thanked Christie for her assistance and left.

The next day, as agreed, we had lunch together. At 11 am, I showed up, and Noora answered the door to me. It was clear she had spent the night there, judging by the onesie she had on. While it covered her legs and boobs, it was impossible not to see the outline of them, and her curves. She decided to cook at home, and we all had to help.

I offered to assist her in making a delicious avocado salad when she was ready, and she said it was fine to make a start right away; though that was difficult for me, given the massive erection, inspired by her, straining to escape the confines of my pants. We nonetheless got going and, when she started chopping the salad ingredients, her butt shook with every slice, prompting my hard-on to expand even more.

"So, tell me how many girlfriends do you have?" she asked.

"None." I grinned. "I am a good boy."

"Yeah, sure," she laughed. "Tell me, Ahmed: is Ibra's problem common with men?"

"I do not know." I shrugged.

"Okay, fine. Let me ask you straight: have you ever cum before you even touched a woman? And don't outsmart me – just answer."

"Actually, I am not a fast cummer," I replied, and, as I finished my sentence, Christie showed up in her underwear.

"No way!" she screamed. "What are you doing here?"

"This is Ibra's friend," Noora answered for me. "Ahmed, this is Christie, Ibra's girlfriend. She spent the night here too."

"So, you are the Ahmed Ibra is talking about!" said Christie.

"How was it last night?" Noora asked her. "Do not worry – Ahmed knows all about it."

"Oh, the same, just more alcohol," sighed Christie.

"Okay, girls," I said, trying to spare Ibra's blushes. "When should we eat?"

"Not yet, in a while," said Christie. "He doesn't get up before two in the afternoon."

In the living room, we as a team agreed to help Ibra. The two girls sat on a big sofa – one in her underwear, and the other in her onesie ... I could not keep my dick down, and I am sure they noticed it.

"Christie, don't you think you should put something on?" Noora asked her.

"I think both of you should," I said. "I do not want Ibrahim to come out and see me with his sexy sister and girlfriend, with virtually no clothes on."

"I do not need his permission to do anything," Noora responded. "But you are right."

It was about 12 pm, and the food was almost ready.

"Girls, why not go and change, and we can talk in the meantime until Ibrahim wakes up," I suggested, and they accepted.

Now I realised that Ibra was not the only one with a problem. Both girls had theirs too – Christie was so hot, and desperate for real sex, while Noora was so sexy, and had been lonely for two years. I did not know if I could help Ibra, or the girls – they all drank, and they all needed good sex.

The girls went to the same room to change, which told me more about them trusting each other, as they were clearly comfortable being naked together. Christie trusted me by default, and I couldn't help but want and desire them both.

"Now, in order to help Ibrahim, we have to know ourselves first, and talk about our personal problems – and no lies!"

"Well," Christie began. "My problem is: I like Ibra, and he wants me to be loyal to him. He is so nice and kind, but his drinking problem is too much, and he insists I should drink with him. Also, his sexual problem is not easy to put up with! As a girl, I have my needs too."

"How do you satisfy yourself?" I asked, my dick flickering back to life.

She looked at Noora before answering.

"Come on, Ahmed – that is not a fair question," said Noora.

"Look, I will answer any question you ask later, but we have to be honest to help your brother."

"I do touch myself," she answered a little bashfully.

"Every night?"

"Yes."

"Have you been with anybody since meeting Ibra?" I asked.

"No."

"Have you ever had sex with another girl?"

"Yes," said Christie.

"Okay, now your turn, Ahmed," said Noora.

"My biggest problem is how to mix feelings, desire and loyalty," I told her.

"Give us an example," she requested.

"All right, then: as a man, I would not be normal if I did not want you both; but as a friend, I know it would hurt Ibrahim."

"Do you have a girlfriend?" asked Noora.

"No."

"Then how do you satisfy yourself?" she went on.

"When the feeling of the moment is there, and I am with a girl, adding sex is an emotion more powerful than love. Let me give you an example: I am sure you both have that feeling now, even though you are not in love, Noora. And Christie is in love, but she can have it too."

"Do you find Noora attractive?" Christie wanted to know.

"Yes, and much more."

"Are you telling me you fancy Noora?" Christie smirked.

"I will answer, if Noora wishes," I responded.

"Christie and I know each other so well that there are no secrets between us."

"Very well, then yes I do fancy Noora – in every position."

"That is enough!" said Noora.

"Look, if I said no, I do not fancy you, you wouldn't believe me, so believe me when I say I do." I drew a breath and fixed her in my gaze. "Now tell us your problem, Noora."

"My problem is drinking and loneliness," she sighed.

"But you do not drink a lot," I reasoned.

"Oh, at night I do."

"Have you too had sex with a woman?" I asked, crossing my legs to camouflage the bulge in my pants.

"Yes."

"And do you watch porn?"

"Yes, I am a big woman, Ahmed, and at my age my sexual desire is at its strongest. But I do not want to be in a bad sexual relationship, so I satisfy myself. Now let me ask you another question: do you fancy Christie?"

"Yes, but in a good way," I answered.

"What do you mean?" asked Christie, who chuckled along with Noora.

"I would love to taste her, but I know she will not give me the chance," I said. "But, girls, I have a request: please let us not judge each other with the way we talked, and let us concentrate on Ibra's problems."

"Agreed!" they said in unison.

At 2 pm, we were all ready, but Ibra was still sleeping, so Christie went to wake him up, while Noora eyed me to see if I was looking at her ass. Around 3 pm, we finally sat down to a lunch of avocado salad with chicken and potatoes. It was delicious and everybody loved it; and, while we ate, I told Ibrahim:

"Ibra, we have agreed that there is to be no drinking today."

"Deal," he replied. "I will follow what you say, my friend."

We chatted, and I started telling stories about the history of women, their beauty and sexuality, and the loyalty people have to each other. Around 6 pm, it was clear that Ibra, Noora and Christie wanted a drink, which broke our agreement.

"I am going home," I told them. "Because you guys are not serious."

"No way – we will not let you go, and you cannot stop us!" giggled Noora, and all of them jumped on me, laughing.

In the scrum of bodies, my hand strayed all over Noora's body and Christie's boobs, with the two girls clearly watching me as I touched them. In such circumstances I simply could not resist, so stayed.

"Okay, Ahmed, let us agree that this will be our last drinking night, except for wine and champagne," said Noora.

She and Ibra kept knocking glass after glass back, and though Christie did not have as much, she still got tipsy. At 9 pm, we watched TV, with Christine sitting next to Ibrahim and Noora lying on a sofa, and me in an armchair. The girls went to change their clothes, returning in cotton nighties that left little to the imagination, revealing the shape of their underwear, and that they were not wearing a bra.

The movie we watched was about a man visiting Africa with his friend and girlfriend. Camping in the jungle, it became clear that, in a weird synergy with Ibra's circumstances, he drank a lot; but was not able to have sex with his girlfriend when she pursued it. The man's friend approached her, but she refused his advances and pushed him away. He was not to be dissuaded, though, pinning her down and, after she relented, removing her panties. But before they could have sex, a tribe from the jungle appeared, killing both men and putting the girl in the tent, naked. The tribe's chief presented her with her boyfriend's head, tossing it next to her, and she kneeled on all fours, realising she had no choice but to cede to his demands. The chief then took her doggy style, and her eyes were full of tears at the pleasure of sex. It was a powerful film and, once it finished, we all sat in silence for a while.

It was clear to me that Noora, lying on the sofa with her dress hitched up above her knees, clinging to her body, was tremendously excited, her pussy beating as if her heart was pounding through it. I was still sitting in the armchair, with my dick struggling to free itself and announce how mad and big it was. Ibra stood up and led a reluctant Christie to his room by the hand, while Noora stood up, drowsy and wet, telling me she needed to go to her room. She almost tripped, so I helped escort her to bed. At least ten times, I felt her body, and she felt my dick hitting her everywhere.

When I put her to bed, we looked at each other, hoping to do something we should not. I gave Noora a quick kiss on the lips and said goodnight, and she told me I was welcome to sleep on the sofa. The minute I left her room, I unzipped my jeans and freed my wang to breathe and announce its revolution. The lights and TV were off. I noticed Christie sitting there in darkness, looking none too happy, and when I sat on the sofa next to her, she noticed my dick.

Her curly hair and watery eyes, and the image of her being all but dragged to Ibra's room to see him cum in a few seconds, made me want to give her the satisfaction she craved. I was planning to pull my pants up, but instead stood in front of her, brought my love truncheon to her lips, and said: "No talk. Do whatever you feel, and I will not speak about it to anyone, even you, Christie."

Being drunk and hungry for sex, having watched that girl getting fucked, and dying to be in her position, Christie said nothing. She popped my dick in her mouth and started sucking it in a nasty, hungry way. When she had finished sucking it, she stood up; and as I lay down on the sofa, she lifted her dress up and sat on me. And then she fucked me for herself in a way that indicated she did not care who was there – she just wanted a hard dick inside her, and in it was. She was so wet; she came in around thirty seconds. I begged her not to stop – to keep moving – holding her hips and helping her move up and down; and a minute or so later, she was squirting and holding her face from screaming. And then she collapsed on top of me, with my cock still inside. "Do not stop," I asked.

"I have to," she mumbled, out of breath. "I am exhausted!"

I was far from exhausted, so I kneeled her on all fours and took her doggy style, just like in the movie, penetrating so deep, and so hard, that it felt as if I was hitting her stomach. She screamed with delight, shoving her ass back against my pelvis, and virtually forcing me to shoot my load. We yelled at the same time, her juices flooding my dick, which fired a stream of hot jism into her. Saying nothing, I lay on the sofa and put Christie on top of me.

"Do not think badly of what happened between us," I whispered, kissing her head. "I believe you are a good girl, and we will not do this again. We will just forget about it." I hugged her, saying: "Shush, just relax," and was so tired, I fell asleep. Waking up at around 7.30 am, I found that I was alone. Since nobody else was up yet, I headed back home and must admit I was afraid that Christie would tell Ibrahim about what we had done.

For three days, I heard nothing from any of them, until Ibra called and said he wanted to see me. Driving to his home, I had manifold thoughts running through my mind, with most alluding to the possibility that Christie had told Ibra about us, and how I would explain myself. But as soon as I got there, he hugged me and said:

"Ahmed, forgive me for being so drunk, and not following the doctor's advice. I do not want to lose a good friend like you, especially now that you have grown closer to Christie and Noora."

Thank God, Christie said nothing, and Ibra thought I was mad at him because of his drinking. Neither of the girls was around at first but after a while, they both arrived wearing sports shorts and tops, sweating from running around the compound; their faces not showing any sign of upset.

"Did I not tell you Ahmed was very nice, and would not be upset with us?" Ibra said to Norma.

Christie stepped towards me, and hugged me, whispering: "Thank you. I did not tell him."

As for Noora ... oh, Noora ... her thighs filled her shorts, while her boobs lifted her shirt in a way that challenged my dick not to stand to attention out of respect for what she had there.

"You also owe him a hug, Noora," Ibra told his sister, who did as he suggested; and, as she did, I pressed my chest onto her boobs.

They all said they liked my cooking and wanted to taste more of it, and I agreed on one condition: that I cook at my home, so I could guarantee no drinking. Both girls went to take a shower and to change, and once they were ready, we left for my place, stopping at a supermarket en route to purchase the ingredients for my dishes. Christie wore a T-shirt that clung to her neck, while Noora's was a tight fit, with buttons.

"You girls get the salad stuff, and I will get the rest," I said.

"Which cucumber do you want?" Noora asked cheekily, to which Christie laughed.

"An English one," I replied.

At home, I asked the girls to make the salad, while I taught them how to cut thinly. As I started cooking, Ibra said he was popping out to buy some cigarettes. After a while, I went to the bathroom in my room, aware that Christie was following me.

"Do not worry, I am a big girl," she said, running her hand over my dick. "I can see how desperate you are to screw Noora."

She left me uncertain as to whether Noora knew what happened and, after dinner, Ibra wanted to go home right away. He clearly wanted a drink, and I tried to make him stay, but he insisted, using tiredness as an excuse. He told the girls that they could stay, but Noora refused to let him go home alone, and asked Christie to go with him. Noora and I sat alone in silence, each of us wanting the other person to say something. Then, at around 10 pm, she started crying. I turned the lights off, the darkness pierced by a sliver of light coming from outside. I approached her and hugged her, asking what was wrong. Sitting side by side on the sofa, her hand slid on top of my dick. She did not grab it, but left it there and, as an expert poacher, I knew this animal was dying to be slaughtered.

Leading Noora to my bedroom, I told her to relax and said I would make her some lemon tea.

"Listen, take your leggings off, as it will make you more relaxed," I said, before leaving the room. I went to the kitchen, made her tea, then returned to my room, noticing she had not removed them. Reaching for her waist, I grabbed them and pulled them down, saying: "You are not a good listener, lady!"

Oh God, I could see her pussy through her underwear, while her hot thighs made me hurt more.

"Why did you shag her?" she asked in a voice that sounded like it wanted to pose a different question – why not me?

"Take your T-shirt off and I will tell you why," I said.
She did.
"Take your bra off and I will tell you why," I said.
She did.
"Take your underwear off and then I will tell you why," I said.

And she did, revealing a clean, hot, hungry pussy. I took my clothes off, saying: "Ask me to fuck you and I will tell you why."

"Please fuck me," said Noora.

I lifted one of her legs up and eased it in slowly, and literally before it was all in, Noora came. Then, when I fully penetrated her, she moaned: "I love your cucumber!"

I kept screwing her slowly – really slowly – and she kept coming – six times – before she turned around to present her ass to me, wanting me to screw her like the girl in the movie; the way Christie told her I had banged her, I am sure.

She was humping me more than I was humping her, with her butt rippling as she slammed it against my stomach. She was close to her seventh orgasm when she kept repeating: "Why did you fuck Christie? Oh, Ahmed, why did you fuck Christie?", and then she came again as I pulled it out and splashed my cum all over her back. Both collapsing, we said nothing until the following morning, when Noora explained that she and Christie were having sex from time to time. Neither were lesbians, but they enjoyed each other's bodies, and Noora wanted Christie to remain in Ibra's life. Noora was generous with Christie, and really loved the idea of Christie being there for her and her brother.

Both girls talked about me and my sexual cravings every time they saw me. Christie told Noora everything that happened between us, and how it happened, when they were having sex, which made Noora want me even more. I was a year away from my graduation, and that year I really did not need to look for a girlfriend, as both girls came to me for sex almost every week, but never together.

Our relationship as a group, including Ibra, did not change. We met up a lot, and many nights I spent the night in Ibra's house, but never slept on the sofa again. Maybe I could not help Ibra with his sexual problem, but I certainly helped the girls. I became a source of relaxation and stress release for them, and they in turn helped him in other ways. And, in my world, he owed me a big THANK YOU for that.

Chapter 6 – Salma

After graduation, I returned home so Americanised, and full of confidence, that I could help instil positive changes in my country. At first, I hated being controlled by my boss. It was a new experience for me, but I slowly learned how to blend into my surroundings.

The '90s were not a very moderate period in Emirates, nor any Arab country for that matter, with a lot of sexual restriction. The Arabic tradition was fully in force, encouraging small-mindedness, so I knew it would be very hard to find someone to penetrate. Initially, no women excited me. I had just returned from the US, where there were all sorts of sex-hungry women, but I gradually started to find all of them sexy. Training courses at work are common after one year of service and my friend, Ali, had to go to Cairo for two months for this purpose. He asked me if I would take his turn because his dad was sick, and he could not leave him alone. Our boss accepted his proposal, and it was agreed that I would go to Cairo in two weeks' time.

Cairo, in Arabic culture, was known as the mother of the entire world. I had been there before and knew it very well. It was a city characterised by poverty, overcrowding and desperation for a better life. The Egyptians there were so poor that they could not afford any meat – not even once a month

– or to buy a new shirt more than once every two years. On the other side of the fence were people so rich they could afford to buy-up an entire street in LA.

I made my plans to stay in a hotel, aware that my course would start at 8.30 am and end at 3 pm every day, except Thursdays and Fridays. Mahmoud was a very nice, gentle Egyptian driver who worked for the company I was employed by. He kept advising me to ditch the hotel in favour of renting an apartment, claiming it would be more relaxing and cheaper, and that I would not have to put up with hotel food; adding that many of my colleagues thought the same.

Mahmoud was 33 years old and a newlywed, having got married a month before in Cairo to a nice girl called Salma, who was 20 years old. We all helped him get married, covering all his expenses. Selma finished high school, but did not go on to university, as she was unable to afford it; but she was a good housewife, who cooked and cleaned for Mahmoud while he was at work, he told us as the big day approached.

One day, Ali told Mahmoud he was sure he was going to miss his bed in Cairo when he went on holiday. Mahmoud joked "do not remind me!" and had to wait for two years before going. The rule in Emirates back then was that its citizens could go on vacation every two years. When we Emiratis gathered, we always used to joke that Salma must be fat and ugly, otherwise she would have a better choice than Mahmoud.

Before leaving for Cairo, Mahmoud came to me, very politely asking if I could take something with me to Salma.

"Sure," I replied. "But I will not go where she lives."

"Of course not, sir," said Mahmoud. "Salma lives in one room, in a house with her mum and dad, and another four brothers and sisters. The day we got married, they emptied the room for us to spend the night in, and I am trying to save money to build my own room." Handing me $100, he went on: "Please give this to Salma."

"No way," I responded. "I will give her a thousand."

"Actually, there is another way you can help: by letting Salma be your housemaid for this period of your course; but; please; I do not want any other Emirati to know."

"Look, Mahmoud, I will need someone to stay overnight, because I am not an outgoing person."

"As long as she has her own room with a key, I do not mind," he added. "Not that I do not trust you, sir, but she would be uncomfortable."

On the plane, I must admit, I regretted that I agreed to have Salma work for me. The image of her being fat and ugly, as we assumed, kept hitting me. I was also concerned that if I brought a woman back with me, she would tell Mahmoud, and then everybody at work would know. I finally decided that I would ask her not to stay overnight, and only clean and cook my lunch before leaving.

After two days in the hotel, I found a nice three-bedroom apartment that was furnished nicely with a TV and a VCR in every room. I called Mahmoud and gave him my address, and he said that Salma would be with me in an hour. I started unpacking my clothes and, of course, my precious porn videos from my suitcase. I also started making a note of all the groceries I needed to buy, which clothes she had to wash, and which clothes she was to take to the dry cleaners.

I heard the doorbell ringing, so went to answer. When I opened the door, I thought the person standing in front of me had got the wrong address. A very pretty young girl, with beautiful skin and big lips, her eyes exuded sexuality; though it was clear that they expressed something else too: a kind of worn-down fatigue, characterised by poverty. Her body was veiled in a loose black dress that revealed nothing of her body, while a hijab covered her hair. It was not the image me and my friends had of Mahmoud's wife.

"Are you Ahmed?" she asked.

"I am, yes," I answered. "Please, come inside."

When we sat down in my living room, she started speaking about Mahmoud, and asking about him. She was very shy, but wanted to talk, and came across very well.

"Is there anything you do not know how to do?" I asked.

"No, I can do everything," said Salma.

At this point, I was having second thoughts about her staying over, but I did not want to insist. I showed Salma to her room and gave her the key to it. She was happy to have her own bed and shower and, I do not doubt, experienced some relief at gaining a little distance from the poverty to which she was accustomed.

"For you," I said, handing Salma $1,000.

"Oh, thank you, sir." She smiled, clearly grateful. "I know Mahmoud sent a hundred dollars, but this will change my parents' life, at least for a while."

"No problem," I smiled back at her. "Now please tell me how much you want me to pay you per month?"

"Anything you wish, sir. You already gave us a lot."

We finally agreed on $200 per month. Salma said that, with the greatest respect, she would not stay over, if I did not mind, and I agreed. We also agreed that she would arrive at 9 am, when I would have left for my course. While I was gone, she would clean and cook for me, and for her family, taking food back to them every day.

I could not stop thinking about how pretty and attractive she was, and how I was dying to see the rest of her – what kind of body was she hiding under that dress? I started attending the course having made my own breakfast, and when I came back my lunch was already there, and the apartment looked very clean and nice. I usually took an afternoon nap, and at night would either watch football, drive around Cairo or go to the hotel lobby and spend some time there, before returning home to enjoy my porn videos.

On Thursdays and Fridays, I had no courses, but Salma did not know that, and on the first Thursday she was there, I heard her in the kitchen. Because she assumed I would not be present, she was not wearing her hijab, and I approached from behind – my God, she had such long hair, reaching beneath her butt.

"Good morning," I said, making her jump.

"But, sir, I thought you were at your course?" She panicked, shyly trying to hide her hair with her hands.

"Leave it as it is," I said bossily. "It is very pretty, and you look like you could be a movie star."

After a few moments of hesitation, she relaxed, and I believe I touched something inside of her by giving her a compliment, which I am sure she missed very much. Wanting to see her body, I asked: "Salma, why are you wearing such a loose black dress? Is Mahmoud asking you to do so?"

"No no, sir!" she cried. "Mahmoud likes and trusts you – it is my choice."

"Look, I want to do something different with you today," I said. "We will go shopping, then I will take you for lunch."

It was not easy for her to understand why, but she must have sensed that I liked her. And, for my part, I continued to wonder what was under that dress.

She put her hijab on again and we went shopping. She chose some jeans, shirts and shoes, and I asked her to try them on. A female sales assistant helped Salma in the changing room, and I was turned on by her size. I could not believe it – 34 on top, and 34-inch hips. She returned to me wearing her old dress, saying her new clothes fitted well, but I insisted she wore them then and there, as we were going to lunch. And so she went and changed again, leaving the dressing room wearing a long-sleeved white shirt, jeans and black shoes, looking sexy with messy long hair.

I lifted her hair up and tied it with a clip that the sales lady had. Now Salma looked so much more attractive with her buttoned shirt and jeans, which perfectly demonstrated the contours of her butt. At lunch, she was shy again and only said a few words, starting every sentence with 'Sir'. It was clear to both of us that I had an interest in her, and that she was afraid of it and very alert, although from time to time, she would be very flattered by my compliments.

"Salma," I said. "There is a lot more that we have to buy for you, especially pyjamas and underwear."

"Oh, I could never accept," she said, her shyness really taking hold. "I could never take such things home to a room shared by everyone else. And I get embarrassed when I talk about these things."

"How is your marriage?" I asked.

"Mahmoud is very nice to me, and loves me, and he really wants to work hard so that we can have our own place."

"That is very good to hear, women should be respected and pleased well in bed. Are you pleased?" I asked.

"Well, we have only had sex once, on the night we got married."

I was really pulling the words from her mouth, as she was so hesitant to talk. "Did you enjoy the sex that night?" She avoided the question, glancing away, so I tried again. "Salma, sex is an important part of a relationship, and there is no need to be so shy about it. We can talk freely."

After several more attempts, Salma finally answered me: "I do not know, but it felt like I was having an electrical shock from head to toe." And, with that, I had my answer.

Later that day, I went to buy some nice pyjamas and underwear for Salma. The next morning, before leaving for work, I purposely left a porn movie playing on the VCR, sensing that when she came to clean, she would watch it. I repeated the process for three days, but she did not talk about it at all; and we did not see each other during that time, as she arrived at the apartment after I left to attend the course, and she left before I came home.

I called Mahmoud back in the Emirates, requesting: "Salma is a very nice girl, and I am happy with her work, but remember I told you I needed someone to stay over, and she politely told me that she cannot, which I understand. So can you please find me somebody who can come after she leaves?"

"Oh no, sir!" he responded. "I insist, you cannot trust anyone other than my wife to take care of you, being so honest and loyal."

"Do not force her if she does not want to, but if she does, I will double her pay."

The next day when I returned home, Salma was there with a small bag, awaiting me. We looked at each other as if we both knew what I was trying to get.

"Do not worry about Mahmoud," I told her. "If you do not wish to stay overnight, you should not feel obliged, and I will still pay you double."

"Sir, to tell you the truth, here is like heaven for me, but I do not think it is right to stay alone with you."

"I agree. But, look: you have your room key and your own bathroom, so you can take a shower whenever you want, and relax and watch movies. I do not normally demand a lot at night – it is only from time to time that I will need something."

That night was full of politeness and respect, and I truly gave her all the confidence she needed. Going to bed, it was not easy to sleep, knowing a sexy girl – who I had no doubt was hungry for another electrical shock – was in the next room. I wanted her so much, and many times I felt compelled to make a stupid excuse to knock on her door, but did not.

In the morning, she was making breakfast in her black dress again, and I told her that this was not allowed anymore, handing her the pyjamas and underwear, and asking that she at least wear them while she was in my apartment. I left the VCR on, with the porn movie playing, and headed to work; and did so again for another two days.

On the third day, I left my course early and headed back home. Letting myself back in as quietly as possible, I made my way to my bedroom, heard the porn movie playing, and eased the door open. My God, she was in a pair of pyjamas – no bra, no underwear – the top to which was wide open, with the pants pulled down. She had two fingers sliding in and out of her pussy, which looked so attractive, with a neat little bush on top.

I know all my porn videos like the back of my hand, and the scene that was on involved a man screwing his friend's wife. I pulled my eyes away from her a few seconds later, closed the door and went into the living room. Ten minutes later, she joined me there, wearing jeans and a T-shirt.

"Sir, would you like me to make you any tea, or something?" she asked.

"Salma, sit down," I said. "I want to talk to you."

She did as I asked, her hands resting on her lap.

"I think you are a lovely girl, Salma. It is not easy for a young girl who has only had sex once not to crave it, and with Mahmoud away, you could have it any time you want. But you are a good girl, and what you did is perfectly right and okay, because you need to satisfy yourself."

"So, you are not upset with me, sir?"

"Not at all and, furthermore, I will give you your own videos to watch in your room."

"How do those women do that?" she wanted to know. "Are they not shy?"

"When people do something for the first time, yes; but then they get used to it."

I did my best to make her feel comfortable, but we both knew she was not – she was so scared that something would happen between us, and I was so scared that it would not. I put another porn movie in her room and, that night, when she returned there, she locked the door. I lingered outside her room for the best part of thirty minutes before hearing, through the keyhole, that she had started to play the film.

Two days later, I changed the movie for her. That night, when she was in her room and started to play it, I could not take it anymore, and knew I had to have her. I knocked on her door and she opened a few seconds later. I could see a few buttons on her top still open as if she had tried to fasten them in a hurry.

"Can I do anything for you, sir?" she asked.

"I was just wondering if you want to change the movie I gave you?"

"No, I am fine," she told me.

She locked her door again, and I went to my room. Five minutes later, at around 9 pm, I returned to her room, knocked on the door and said: "Please come to my room – I need help."

She came in her pyjamas, and I told her I needed to arrange my books on a shelf. Every time she bent over to take the books and put them on the shelf, I threw them back on the floor. We were both silent and, realising it would not be an easy night for her if I continued, I stopped and let her place the books on the shelf.

"Is there anything else, sir?" she asked.

"Yes, I want you to call Mahmoud," I said, dialling his number and asking to talk to him.

He was so happy to talk to her, and I asked him to take his time, without worrying about the bill. During their conversation, I started touching her. At first, she looked at me, shocked, which made me touch her even more. I hugged her from behind, and she felt my dick rubbing up against her ass as I played with her nipples. Mahmoud was on the line, talking about saving for their future, and I started touching her pussy from behind. It was crazy wet – literally soaking – and she gave me another look, as if to say: please do not ... or at least not now.

"Salma, can you hear me?" came Mahmoud's voice from the other end of the line.

"Yes," she replied, and then, in one move, I pulled her pants down, bent her over a chest of drawers, and started banging her. Our eyes met in the mirror capturing us at it, and watching me screw her made her go wild. I continued to thrust into her as she spoke to him and whispered in her ear: "Tell him I am fucking you." It made her lose her mind, and she came while talking to him. Shivering and shaking, she told Mahmoud that she would have to end the call because she was cooking.

When she hung up, I took her to bed and removed all her clothes. She said nothing at all and, lifting both of her legs up, I saw her pussy pulsating between them, with that soft thatch of hair on top. I slid all my dick inside her and screwed her hard, seeing the joy in her eyes with every hit. There was no talk; we just looked at each other, eye to eye and dick to pussy. The only noise she made was a lengthy "Ahhhhhh!" as she came, followed by mine after pulling it out and splashing my hot screw glue all over her body. Salma's nipples were so hard, and her boobs like a mid-size pomegranate – my favourite fruit to eat, and my favourite juice to drink.

Living a very hard life, struggling to survive and having only tasted sex once, knowing she would have to wait for at least two years before it happened again, had proved too much for her; as had seeing all of those girls in the porn films enjoying the benefits of a hard cock, seeing my hungry eyes fixated on her, and the shock of Mahmoud allowing her to sleep over at my place, with the stupid condition of her having her own room key.

There was no doubt that Salma's two-month stay with me changed her entire perspective as a woman. Having been raised in a society where women were regarded as a man's property – to serve him, cook for him, have his children, and obey his commands – she had been shown that a woman can be respected as a beautiful soul, not just as an object, be looked after, made to feel appreciated – special even – and have her sexual desires fulfilled. The time we spent together transformed her vision of life, broadened her horizons, and changed the way she would allow Mahmoud to treat her, which gave them a far better chance of a happy marriage, and long life.

Chapter 7 – Sara

In 1997, I worked so hard to make money. My dad wanted me to take care of everybody in our family as our money situation was not that good. Business in Emirates was steady, mostly relying on real estate. I used to go to every government department, especially the planning unit, trying to gain approval for some architectural plans and building permits. I used to buy land, plan for it in a different way than was typical in Emirates, then sell it for more, or build on it and sell it after. It was the beginning of the nation's female revolution of showing in public and working in professions other than teaching, and in every government department, there was a designated area for women, where men were not allowed to enter. Even banks had their own female-only branches, which would only hire and serve women.

Back then, I lived alone with all my memories from Colorado – the snow, the simple, real life, and the type of women I liked. Life was not easy for me, and the only thing stopping me from going back was my dad and his high expectations of me taking care of everyone. I used to work two shifts: for the government in the morning, and in my small office in the afternoon, and I lived alone in a three-bedroomed villa.

At that time, your best chances of hunting success were the Filipinos who worked in restaurants or shops, or some ladies from Lebanon or Syria, who worked in doctors' clinics and private companies. But, for sure, life was very restricted and when somebody dated a girl, they would drive to the desert, simply because Emirates was very small, and everybody knew everybody, and they did not want to be seen together.

The dating rules there were standard: a man was free to kiss and touch a single woman, and brush their dick against their pussy, but sex was not permitted unless it was within the confines of a marriage. One day, at the planning department, following a building permit application, the employee asked me to take my application to the next room. By mistake, I entered the female-only section. All of the women and I were shocked, and I could not believe what I saw, and that I was still in Emirates – no abayas, no hijabs, full make-up, dressed as if they were going to a party, different hairstyles and lengths, with many hiding and others screaming at me to get out.

I stood where I was, not wishing to move; looking at them until one of them came to me. With short dark hair and sharp eyes, she showed a lot of what I was looking for – big boobs, a very tiny waist, and a full butt; I would say 36-26-40 and about 165cm, wearing an off-white suit and a white T-shirt. She was clearly very confident in herself and asked, in English: "Are you sure you are in the right place?"

"I am sure I am not in the wrong place," I told her.

"You had better leave," she said, without seriousness in her voice.

Honestly, this girl touched everything in me. I liked her a lot, and felt as if I had found what I was missing in Emirates: so sexy, fluent in English, not shy at all and, when she looked me in the eyes, I felt as if she was telling me 'Oh, so you like me, do you?' Before I left, I said: "What is your name and number?"

She told me her name was Sara, and she gave me the department number, before repeating that I had to leave. It was about 12 noon, and jobs back then ended at 12.30. That afternoon I went home so happy, and so impatient for the following day, so that I could call Sara. I could not scrub from my mind the image of her smiling and looking at me, and numerous thoughts ran through my head, picturing what we could do together. At 9 am the next morning, I called and asked for Sara.

"This is Sara speaking," she replied.

"I am Ahmed from yesterday," I told her, and we started talking in English.

"Did you really enter our department by mistake?" she asked.

"Look, I want to see you," I said.

She laughed. "You are crazy!"

"Yes, I am, and I want to see you now," I said.

The planning department back then was in a single-storey building, and there was a backdoor access for the women.

"Come to the back door, and I will pop out and say hello," said Sara.

Within twenty minutes, I was waiting outside, and my eyes were looking in all directions, hoping that nobody saw me waiting there, wondering what I was doing. Sara came out in a light brown suit and off-white T-shirt, and climbed into my car. As she smiled, her confidence shone through.

"I can drive around, or we can go to my place and talk there if you would sooner. There, we would be safer from prying eyes."

"Look, I am single," she smiled. "And you are not going to have sex with me."

"You know I love how you are," I started to explain. "And you took a piece of my mind and heart, but how did you become like that? You are so different and look like you lived outside Emirates."

Driving around and talking in the car, Sara spoke about herself. Her dad studied in the USA and when he had her, he raised her the way he believed was right, and now he depended upon her in his business. He insisted that she become the way she was and did not mind what other people had to say. She also believed that most women would be like her if given the chance – and, indeed, this is a common sight now.

"Can I kiss you please?" I asked, kissing her on the lips before she had a chance to answer.

"Do you not think you should give me your number?" she smiled.

I gave her my number, and she went back to work. Driving back home, I was so happy to know Sara, and felt that, through her, I could love Emirates. I did not know whether I loved her, wanted to have sex with her, or both. I spoke to her daily at around 7 pm, exchanging thoughts and opinions on life. She loved my wisdom and trusted me straight away. I loved her trusting me, and I loved her sexuality and the way she looked.

For a month, I kept returning to Sara's work, to chat at the back door. Our kisses became deeper and more passionate, and I loved tasting her tongue, touching her body, and grabbing her hand to put on my dick. Her birthday was impending, so I asked her what she wanted. She smiled and said underwear! Sara was loving how naughty she could be with me; I believe she found in me what I found in her, but even though she was single, there was no chance for me to be inside her.

While talking via phone on a Tuesday afternoon, Sara said: "I have taken tomorrow off from work."

"Why?" I asked.

"I was planning to drive around with you and talk."

"Well, that sounds good to me," I said, glad that she wanted to spend more time with me. We agreed that I would meet her at her work at 9 am, with her driver dropping her off there, to return at 11.30 am to pick her up, which would give us two-and-a-half hours to spend together. "Sara, until now, I did not have the chance to talk to you eye to eye, as we always sat beside each other in the car. And, honestly, I want to touch you. I know you are single, so I promise I will not have sex with you ... but I cannot promise I will not do other things."

I kept talking sexually to her, describing how she could suck me off and ride me with her underwear on, until she came. I went on: "Sara, my closet door is mirrored, so I will lay down on the floor, with my head towards the door, and you can ride me and watch yourself in the mirror."

"I will be at work by eight, so why wait until nine?"

I took this as a yes for coming to my home, and said: "I will come at eight, then."

"Do not have breakfast – we will cook together," she said.

Knowing that that was the best I would get from our phone call, we hung up and I prepared to meet her the following day. When she came to meet me, she wore a maroon Juicy Couture tracksuit with a black shirt, and her Abaya on top. She looked so cute, pretty, and sexy, smiling, and not having any fear. She wore just a little lipstick – enough to give her lips some shape, and nowhere near enough to stop me from kissing them.

Kissing her, I asked: "How old you are, Sara?"

"Twenty-four," she answered. "As you know, I am single and, as you also know, I will keep my promise and not have sex with you ... but I will also keep my other promise of doing everything else."

From Sara's strong, confident personality, I was sure that while she would claim to want to resist my advances, as most single women said, she secretly longed for a stiff dick to play with. I had no doubt that I would suck her boobs and put my dong in between them; and that I would brush it against her pussy, which I was sure would be tight and devoid of a bush. I must admit that my mind was full of thoughts alluding to that pussy of hers scratching my dick as it moved in and out of her, and the feeling of her butt hitting my tummy while whacking it in doggy style.

After picking her up, she asked: "Where is the kitchen, Ahmed? I am hungry."

"So am I," I said, spinning her around and kissing her on the lips.

We kissed for five minutes on the sofa, and she was so skilled at it, and so passionate. I took her black T-shirt off, saying: "Your bra is more than enough."

Without any hesitation, she accepted and, in her pants and bra, and me in a sports shirt and no underwear, we made breakfast in the kitchen.

"Have you ever cooked cheese with eggs?" she asked.

"No," I said.

"It is really yummy – I will make it for you."

I made some tea with saffron, rosewater and cardamom, while Sara cooked breakfast. While eating, I said: "Sara, do you know you have brought my soul back to me?"

"Are you not worried that I will take it back from you?" she grinned.

"Well, it is my soul's choice who it wants to be with." I laughed. "Sara, you are a wonderful girl – so open-minded, beautiful, and sexy. It does not make sense that you are single."

"Is this a proposal?" she asked.

I fell silent, and then she laughed, raising one eyebrow, and saying: "Ahmed, I never thought for a second that you will marry me." She checked the time, saying: "Oh my God, time is flying. It is ten am already. Remember, I must return by half-eleven! To me, it sounds like you do not want to taste me before I leave?"

"Sara, let me show you my bedroom," I said, heading to the first floor, with Sara in front of me.

The way her butt moved in her tight pants made her irresistible to me, and she sat on the bed, facing my mirrored closet.

"So, you were not joking about the mirrored doors!"

"No, I was not," I said, kissing her on the lips.

I then licked her tongue and took her bra off, her boobs announcing their freedom. They looked so round, with a brown, one inch circle surrounding her nipples. I asked her to stand up and face the mirror, and came from behind to hug her. We looked in the mirror for a few seconds before I started pulling her pants down.

"Take my clothes off and hug me from behind!" she demanded.

We were both naked, except for her underwear, my dick was hard, and she loved it hitting her back. Side to side, next to the mirror, she kneeled down and took my dick in her hand. Then, like a baby who had not been fed for a week, she started sucking it. From time to time, she spat on it and sucked it again, but I asked her to stop and lay in bed, to watch me standing with my dick, so hungry for what she was not allowed to have.

While doing this, she started touching herself and rubbing her fingers on top of her underwear. Unable to hold on anymore, I started brushing my dick on top of her knickers. She was so desperate for it, and I was ten times more desperate than she was. No Emirati would think for a second of having sex with a single girl, as the entire country would know, and they would be forced to marry – a story that repeated itself year after year for anyone who did it.

I lay on the floor, with my head towards the door, and said: "Come and screw me, bad girl, I want to hear you coming."

She straddled me, moving her covered pussy on my cock while looking in the mirror and watching my big dick wanting to occupy her. Feeling it rubbing on her pussy, she came with a joyous yelp, covering her mouth with her hands.

"I love you," she said as she bent to kiss me. "How is it that you have not cum?"

I took her back to bed, laid her on her tummy and started rubbing my dick against her bottom. I was ready to explode, which she felt, saying: "Do it! Do it please!"

I came all over her back, and my spunk drifted onto the right side of her waist. It was about 11.15 am, and we had just had almost an hour's worth of sexual lust, passion, and all kinds of mind control from both of us. There was no time to take a shower, so I asked her not to move and brought her a hot towel, which I used to clean her back. We kissed, and quickly headed to the car.

"It was not easy, not to fuck you," I said.

Without any fear or warning, she said: "That is the rule, and you will follow it. And next time, I will visit you, and you do not have to come to work anymore."

"How can you do that?" I asked. "Your driver will know."

"Do not worry, he has been my driver since I was twelve years old, and he would never talk."

The image of Sara and her body, and her eyes when she came, kept me hot all day. I could not believe how confident she was of herself, and how she trusted me with the most precious thing an Arab girl could have – her virgin pussy.

I must admit, there were many moments when the devil inside me encouraged me to bang her, but the consequences of being found out were so punishing that I was stopped in my tracks. We talked that night, with practically all of our conversation centring on the time we shared together, the way we kissed, the way she sucked me, her eyes coming before her pussy did, the way I scratched my dick on her pussy, and the feeling of my cum drifting to the right side of her.

"I do not like you trusting me ninety-nine percent though," I said.

"What do you mean?" she asked.

"You should have taken your underwear off and trusted that I would not screw you, as I promised."

Without a moment's hesitation, she came back at me: "Next time, I will, but I want to watch you licking it in front of the mirror."

I could barely contain the swell in my pants, which rose like a shark hunting prey. It was Tuesday, and I told her: "I have to go to Dubai on Friday and come back on Sunday."

"I will come and see you on Thursday, then," she said.

"No, please – come tomorrow."

"I start work at eight am, so can come at six, spend an hour with you, get ready and head to work."

The following morning, I got up early, wanting to ensure I was ready for Sara's arrival. I took a shower, slung a fresh pair of pants on, and donned a pair of jeans and T-shirt. At 5.45 am, the doorbell rang, and there she was, looking fresh and sexy in leggings and crop top. Perhaps I should have given her a little more by way of conversation, but with so little time to spend with her, I led her to my room. Easing her back on my bed, I peeled her clothes off until she was totally naked, and we slid under the covers.

"Why not see who can resist the other?" I suggested, but she started touching my throbber before I could make my move – which I longed to do, but wanted to see her strike first.

"You win," she said unashamedly and went down to suck me so hungrily and so naughtily, spitting on my dick and licking it with passion.

My toes were touching the lips of her pussy, which felt so wet and hungry. I took her in front of the mirror and started licking her as she desired.

"Oh, fuck – that is so good!" she wailed to herself. "I am such a bad girl! He is licking me! I am cumming!"

As she screamed with passion, I tasted the fruity, salty flavour of her juices. Holding onto my hair, she said: "I hate you! You control me in and out, and you make me cum so easily!"

I took Sara back to bed, kissed her tongue to tongue, sucked her nipples and started rubbing my hard dick against her pussy. The head of my dick hovered above her pussy, and the rest rubbed it. I was peering into her eyes, and she was clearly close to her second orgasm.

"Please allow me to put just half an inch in," I begged.

"Okay, just a little," she said.

When I did, she almost fainted, and mumbled: "I am married, but please do not put it all in."

I could not tell if she was being genuine or not, but as I slipped a little more in, she helped feed a bit more.

"NO – NO!" she moaned while gyrating her hips, helping to ease me in fully.

She had a tight pussy, which made me harder; and I screwed her with everything I had, reacting to her every moan to try and satisfy her. Sara came twice before taking me to the mirror to ride me the way she loved – but for real this time.

I cannot cum quickly with a girl on top, but Sara was getting wetter every second and, I swear to God, she came, like, six or seven times before collapsing on top of me, saying she did not have any energy left, and asking how I could not have cum yet. Bending her over, I started taking her from behind in front of the mirror, so that we could watch each other at it, making it look more like the porn movie that had been playing in our minds ever since we met. Before cumming, I pulled my dick out and, as she watched via the mirror, shot my load on her butt, her back, and my carpet.

We both went to my room and fell into bed, spent. I hugged her from behind, and for fifteen minutes we said nothing; then she started telling me her story. Sara got married to her cousin five years before, he was so good to her at first and she really loved him, and they had two kids: a boy, Ali, and a girl, Mariam. She loved sex and watched a lot of porn with her husband while at it. She would not tell me to whom she was married, nor her full name, but she knew very well who I was.

Two years earlier, something happened with her husband, and he could not get an erection. Sara tried helping him, but it did not work, so she asked him to see a doctor, and he only agreed a month before I met her. His inability to bang her, and his knowledge of how sexual she was, made him feel that she might screw somebody else, but she never did. That is why she kept telling me she was single, and why her pussy was so tight.

I was expecting Sara to say she was sorry for having sex with me, but the truth is that she was not. She kept coming to my place every other day for two years, her driver dropping her off at 6 am to take her doctor's injection. She was perfect for my needs: a very good-looking, sexy woman who I could bang without any responsibility, though in reality, I believe I was Sara's sex slave. A very strong lady with a great personality, who had a husband and kids, Sara was defeated by herself, not by me.

She was overconfident and so sure she could enjoy our time together without falling for me. She did so well, and she tricked me, and she got exactly what she wanted, how she wanted it. When the feeling of that moment was there, the power of her mind started challenging all of her principles, and in that second, her brain sped through years of thought: her husband's knowledge of her high sexuality and desire; him not dealing with his problem seriously, because he was sure she was loyal and had no other choices; regarding his problem as hers too; and, most of all, the sexual foreplay we enjoyed, without penetration.

All that was in Sara's brain when an inch of my cock was inside her. Her last weapon to use on me was her revelation that she was married, and leave it to me to decide, hoping I would not have sex with her but actually begging me to do so. Sara released all those years of anger and frustration on me and, as a strong as she was, she loved the sex servant games we played, and how I satiated her sexual hunger.

It was only then that she finally became more understanding of her husband's problem, and was more supportive, which resulted in him seeking a doctor's advice. Her thoughts were clearer and more directed towards her family, and her loving husband; and the time we spent together undoubtedly helped free her mind to focus on them, since she was taking care of her sexual needs, which had been ignored, and subsequently held her back.

Final Words

Treason ... what is it? We may find hundreds of different definitions in this word, but the simplest is that it is the enjoyment of a sincere emotion, through which we find our lost soul; and where, seconds later, we are left with the feeling of remorse for what we did, based simply on the concept of life, which was passed on to us by our ancestors.

It is not necessarily the case that when one falls for the desires of a random person, that they are unhappy in their daily life ... but surely one has found something missing in their life, within their relationship. It is not just the sex, but the sensations and feelings that are stirred and awakened within that woman, before she falls into the sexual act. That act is the easiest part of any betrayal because it responds to what began to grow in the woman's soul and stirs her innermost feelings, before falling into 'forbidden' sex.

Why should we feel guilty and ashamed after doing something with the utmost sincerity, fuelled by feelings that give us pleasure? Do we have to be clear to the other party about what we did? And if betrayal gives this pleasure, do we always have to do it? Of course, we must not confront the partners of those whose wives have strayed because they will not be able to understand either the act itself nor the feelings that led to the so-called 'forbidden' sex. Their thinking will stop at the sex act itself, and not the reasons that triggered their wives to take this road.

The feelings which repeatedly come to life during those sexual acts are completely outside of our human control. They exude beauty, and arrive with such power and authenticity that they are totally incomparable to any other emotion, reviving us and bringing us back to life.

The spirit of this book objects to the idea of a betrayal, viewing it instead as nothing but following the feelings of the moment, extracted by a very skilful master, and fulfilling the deepest desires that one misses, and longs for in a relationship – sometimes for many years.